THE BOBBSEY TWINS
By Laura Lee Hope

THE BOBBSEY TWINS
IN VOLCANO LAND

"You've hit something!" Flossie cried

The Bobbsey Twins
in Volcano Land

By

LAURA LEE HOPE

GROSSET & DUNLAP

Publishers   *New York*

PRINTED IN THE UNITED STATES OF AMERICA

The Bobbsey Twins in Volcano Land

CONTENTS

THE BOBBSEY TWINS
IN VOLCANO LAND

CHAPTER I

A MYSTERIOUS TREASURE

"MAY we borrow your teakettle, Dinah?" six-year-old Flossie Bobbsey asked, her blue eyes dancing with mischief.

"What you want my kettle for?" Dinah asked suspiciously.

"Freddie and I are going to make a volcano," Flossie explained, "like the ones in Hawaii!"

Dinah rolled her eyes toward the ceiling in mock despair. "Ever since Lani came, all I hear is volcanoes!"

Lani Kahakua, a pretty little Hawaiian girl of ten, had come to Lakeport with her foster parents, Mr. and Mrs. Frank Carson, to visit the Bobbseys. Mrs. Carson and the twins' mother had gone to school together.

"Mr. Carson is a vol-can-ol-'gist," Flossie said carefully, "and he knows all about volcanoes. Please let us have the kettle," she added pleadingly.

Dinah Johnson, fat and jolly, helped Mrs. Bobbsey with the housework, and her husband, Sam, drove a truck for Mr. Bobbsey's lumber business. The office and yard were located on the shore of Lake Metoka, in Lakeport, where the Bobbseys lived.

The kindly colored woman smiled. "All right, honey child," she said. "You take the kettle, but bring it back when you're through with it."

"I will. Thank you, Dinah," the little girl said, and filled the kettle with water.

Outside, around the picnic grill, were Lani, and the other Bobbsey children—Flossie's twin, Freddie, who had tousled yellow hair, and the twelve-year-old twins, Bert and Nan, who had dark eyes and hair.

"Did you get it?" Freddie asked excitedly. Then, seeing the kettle in her hand, he said, "Bert and I have the fire started. It shouldn't take long for the volcano to begin steaming!"

At this point, brown-eyed Lani spoke up. "I'm afraid the kettle is not going to look much like a real volcano. Can't we cover it with something?"

Freddie cried, "I know! I'll be back!" With that he dashed into the house.

In a short while he returned, his arms full.

"Oh, that's wonderful!" Nan exclaimed. "The mountains from your electric-train set!"

"Good for you, Freddie," Bert agreed. "They're asbestos and won't burn."

Carefully he placed the asbestos mountains around the teakettle until only the lid and the spout showed above them. Then the children stepped back to look.

"It's great!" Lani applauded. "It is *Kilauea Iki,* little Kilauea. Kilauea is a volcano on my island."

As Lani spoke, a boy about Bert's age strolled into the yard. He was the same height as the Bobbsey boy, but heavier, and usually had a scowl on his face.

"Hello, Danny," Bert said. "What's on your mind?"

Danny Rugg was in Bert and Nan's class at school. His greatest delight seemed to be to play mean tricks on the Bobbseys, and all the children considered him a bully.

"Nothing's on my mind," Danny answered. "What're you making there?" He nodded toward the fireplace.

"We're building a volcano," Flossie explained proudly. "This is Lani. She's from the volcano land of Hawaii."

"A volcano? Huh! It looks like an old teakettle to me," Danny sneered, ignoring the introduction.

"Let's put some grass around the bottom of the mountain," Lani suggested.

When the children bent over to pick the grass, Danny casually swung his foot. *Splash! Hiss!*

A flying ember landed on Lani's bare leg

The teakettle tipped over, spilling the water and putting out the fire. A flying ember landed on Lani's bare leg.

"Ouch!" she cried, jumping up and brushing off the tiny spark.

"That was a mean trick, Danny Rugg!" Bert cried. "You get out of this yard, and quick!"

"Okay, okay," Danny muttered. "Can't any of you Bobbseys take a joke?" With that, he ran off down the driveway.

"Don't worry, Bert," Lani said soothingly. "It didn't hurt me." Then she giggled. "Kilauea erupted. That means Pele is angry with Danny!"

"Who is Pele?" Nan asked Lani curiously.

Before the Hawaiian girl could answer, Bert made a suggestion. "Why don't we all go down to the Soda Shop? I'll treat you to some ice cream. And Lani can tell us about Pele."

"Goody!" Flossie exclaimed. "Come on, everybody!" She started to run down the driveway. Suddenly she stopped. "I forgot something," she explained. "I'll catch up with you."

Quickly Flossie ran back, picked up the teakettle and carried it to the kitchen. Then she followed the others.

The Soda Shop was a favorite meeting place for the young people of Lakeport. But now it was almost empty. Danny and his pal Jack Westley sat at a table, and a lone man was drinking coffee in one of the booths.

Lani and the twins sat down in the next booth. Bert was on one side with the small twins, and Lani and Nan slid onto the other seat.

The children gave their orders, then Nan turned to Lani. "Now please tell us about Pele," she asked.

The little Hawaiian girl looked serious. "Pele is the goddess of volcanoes," she explained. "The Polynesian people have a legend that she makes her home in Kilauea on our island of Hawaii. When she becomes angry, she can make the volcano erupt."

"Who are Pol-nesiums?" Flossie wanted to know.

Lani smiled. "I am a Polynesian," she replied. "My ancestors lived on islands in the South Pacific Ocean. One of these islands was Tahiti. Hundreds of years ago, several tribes of people left there, led by chiefs. They traveled in large sailing canoes to the Hawaiian islands. I am descended from one of those early chiefs," she ended proudly.

"Oh, Lani!" Nan sighed. "How romantic!"

Lani looked sad. "My mother and father lost their lives three years ago when they were out sailing and a bad storm came up. Ever since then I've lived with the Carsons, who were great friends of my parents. I miss my mother and father terribly, but Aunt Jane and Uncle Frank have been wonderful to me!"

Nan patted Lani's hand. "We're so sorry about your parents," she said softly. "It's good you have your aunt and uncle."

"Tell us more about Pele," Flossie urged, taking another spoonful of her ice cream.

"I have a very precious treasure," Lani confided, "which is sacred to Pele. I am the last of my family, and the treasure has come down to me."

"What is it, Lani?" Freddie asked, his eyes shining with excitement.

"I'll show it to you when we get home," the Hawaiian girl promised. "I take it with me whenever I leave Hawaii because"—Lani giggled—"I think it brings me good luck."

Just then there came a rude laugh from the table where Danny and Jack were seated. "What stories some people swallow!" Danny said loudly. Jack snickered in agreement.

The Bobbseys ignored the two boys. "That ice cream was awf'ly good, Bert," said Flossie. "Thank you."

The others echoed her and scrambled out of their seats. When Bert walked past the next booth he noticed that the man seated there was scowling. He was very tanned and had a mop of coarse black hair. He wore thick dark glasses.

When Bert reached the door, he happened to look back. The tanned stranger had moved to Danny and Jack's table and was talking to the boys. "That's odd," Bert told himself. "I wonder who he is."

When the children reached the Bobbsey home, Lani ran upstairs and soon came down again carrying something in her hand. "Here's my treasure," she said.

Freddie looked at it, then said in disappointment, "Why, it's just a stone!"

"Yes, but it's a Pele stone," Lani explained. "My parents were sure that it was once in the shape of Pele herself, but it has been handled by so many people through the years it's hard to tell that now."

She placed the stone on the hall table, and the children bent over it with interest. It was about the size of a man's fist and of reddish color. As they examined the object, it seemed to be surrounded by a soft glow.

"I think it's bee-yoo-ti-ful!" Flossie cried. "May I hold it?"

The twins took turns handling the strange stone. Then Lani carried it up to her room again. That evening the conversation at the dinner table was entirely about Hawaii.

"Your work at the Hawaiian Volcano Observatory must be very interesting," slender, pretty Mrs. Bobbsey observed with a smile, looking at Mr. Carson.

"Indeed it is," the blond, husky scientist replied.

"Tell us more about volcanoes, Mr. Carson," Freddie begged. "I'm very interested in fires." Ever since Freddie was a little boy he had said he was going to be a fireman when he grew up. His favorite plaything was a toy fire engine.

Freddie grinned as his tall, handsome father laughed and said, "That's right. Freddie's my little fat fireman!"

"Well," Mr. Carson admitted, "volcanoes do cause fires, but we have such a good warning system on Hawaii that there is very rarely any loss of life. In fact, the eruptions of our volcanoes are tourist attractions. People come from all over the world to watch them."

"That would be great fun!" Bert remarked. "I'd sure like to see an eruption sometime."

"Come to Hawaii and you may have the opportunity," Mr. Carson replied with a smile. "We have two volcanoes on our island which still blow their tops now and then!"

"What are their names?" Nan asked.

"Mauna Loa and Kilauea," was the reply.

"Hawaii sounds fabulous!" Nan said. "We've been studying about it in school."

"The volcanoes are interesting," Mrs. Carson said, "but I think you children would also like all the water sports, especially at Waikiki Beach."

"Is that near where you live?" Flossie asked.

Mrs. Carson explained that Waikiki Beach was part of the city of Honolulu, which was on the island of Oahu. "There are really eight islands in the Hawaiian chain," she explained. "The one on which we live, Hawaii, is called the Big Island because it's the largest. It's also known as Volcano Island since it's the only one which still has active volcanoes."

"You'd like Waikiki," Lani put in. "That's where everyone has fun with surfboards and outrigger canoes."

"Those outriggers must be keen!" Bert said enviously. "I wish we had one!"

Mr. Carson looked at him. "I shouldn't think it would be too difficult to build one, Bert. Have you a regular canoe?"

Bert's eyes sparkled. "Yes. We keep one at the lumberyard dock. You mean we could change it to an outrigger?" he asked eagerly.

"Certainly," Mr. Carson answered. "Want to work on it tomorrow morning?"

It was agreed that Bert and Freddie would take Mr. Carson to the lumberyard. The twins' father said he had just the right lumber for the outrigger. "Maybe you'll start a fashion for outriggers on Lake Metoka," he remarked jokingly.

Next morning Bert and Freddie were at the breakfast table early, eager to start work on the canoe. Finally everyone had appeared but the little Hawaiian girl.

"Where is Lani?" Mrs. Bobbsey asked in concern. "Have you seen her this morning, Nan?"

"No, Mother. I'll go up and get her."

Nan had just risen from the table when Lani appeared in the doorway. She was shaking and her dark eyes were swollen from crying.

"My Pele stone is gone!" she sobbed. "My treasure's missing!"

CHAPTER II

AN OUTRIGGER UPSET

LANI'S treasure missing! The Bobbseys looked at one another in dismay.

"When did you have it last?" Mrs. Carson asked Lani kindly. "Perhaps you've just mislaid it."

"Oh no, Aunt Jane," Lani protested. "I showed the Pele stone to the twins yesterday and then put it on the window sill. It was there last night when I went to bed. Now it's gone!" Her eyes filled with tears once more.

"Don't worry, Lani," Nan said reassuringly. "We'll find the stone for you."

"That's right," Freddie spoke up. "We Bobbseys are good detectives. We found Pickaxe's garnet in THE MYSTERY CAVE."

"Yes," Flossie agreed, "and we caught a thief when we went to LONDON TOWER."

Mr. and Mrs. Bobbsey looked at each other and smiled. "The twins do seem to have a talent for solving mysteries," their mother said. "I'm sure they'll unravel this one!"

"In that case, let's get busy," Bert suggested. "Lani says the Pele stone disappeared from her window sill. None of us took it, so it must have been someone from outside."

"But how would anyone get in the house?" Flossie asked in bewilderment.

"We'll find out. You and Nan search for clues in Lani's room," Bert directed. "Freddie and I will look around the yard."

The two boys ran outside to a spot under Lani's window. "Look!" Bert pointed.

There was a flower bed on that side of the house, but now the flowers were trampled and broken. "Oh boy!" Freddie exclaimed. "Someone sure has been here!"

Bert dropped to his knees and carefully examined the ground under the window. There were two depressions about two inches square in the soft dirt.

"What are they, Bert?" Freddie asked, curious.

"It could have been a ladder. Let's see if there are any other signs."

Excitedly the boys scanned the area. Then Freddie discovered the tracks. There were two long trails through the grass about a foot and a half apart. They led to the rear of the yard.

"You're right, it was a ladder!" Freddie cried.

"The thief dragged the ladder all the way to the bushes!"

Bert and Freddie began to push the shrubbery aside in search of the ladder. Suddenly Bert called, "Here it is!"

Together the two boys dragged the ladder out onto the lawn and looked it over. As Bert walked around he suddenly spied something.

"Look at this!" he exclaimed. On the safety brace of the ladder were the stenciled letters: RUGG.

"Danny!" Freddie cried. "We might have known he did it!"

Bert looked grim. "Well, if he did, this time Mr. Danny Rugg's going to get what he deserves!"

Danny's home was not far away and in a few minutes the two Bobbsey boys were running up the Ruggs' front walk. Danny came around the corner of the house.

"What do you want?" he asked in an unfriendly manner.

"We want Lani's Pele stone!" Bert demanded hotly. "We know you took it, so don't try to deny it!"

"I don't know what you're talking about. You're crazy!" Danny protested.

"You left your ladder right in our yard!" Freddie backed up his big brother.

At this moment Mrs. Rugg came out onto the

porch. "Did I hear you say something about our ladder, Freddie? Have you found it?"

"Y-yes. It's in our back yard." Freddie was confused.

"I wonder how it got there," Mrs. Rugg said in surprise. "We missed the ladder from our garage last evening and I've had Danny running all over the neighborhood looking for it."

"See!" Danny said triumphantly. "I had nothing to do with your old rock!"

Bert and Freddie were embarrassed that they had accused Danny unjustly. They apologized and offered to help him carry the ladder back to the Rugg garage. When this had been accomplished Bert and Freddie reported their morning's discovery to the others waiting at the Bobbsey house.

"You'd better call Captain Roscoe, Bert," Mr. Bobbsey advised. "Tell him about the theft of Lani's stone and the ladder that you found." Then turning to Mr. Carson, he added, "I'll see you and the boys later at the lumberyard, Frank."

Bert called Lakeport police headquarters and talked to his friend Captain Roscoe. "We'll send a man out right away, Bert," the officer said.

Two policemen came and made an investigation. They also got a full description of the Pele stone and asked Lani why she thought anyone would want to steal it.

"My stone is very rare," Lani answered. "I guess it's valuable."

After the men had gone, the family had breakfast, although Lani could eat little. Then Mr. Carson, Bert, and Freddie set out for the lumberyard on the shore of Lake Metoka. Sam welcomed them. "I got just the thing for you," he said with a big smile. "A nice flexible piece of wood."

Sam had placed the Bobbseys' canoe in a sort of cradle on the dock, and now the two boys set to work under Mr. Carson's direction. They cut the piece of lumber to a length a little shorter than the canoe, then fastened two smaller pieces to each end of it and hooked them over the side of the canoe. These held the longer piece out about three feet, parallel to the canoe.

Suddenly Freddie cried, "Ouch!" He stuck one finger in his mouth and started dancing about.

"What's the matter?" Mr. Carson asked, putting down his measuring stick and walking over to the little boy.

"I hammered my thumb!"

Mr. Carson chuckled. "Well, I never built anything in my life without hitting my fingers at least once. You have to get used to that if you're going to do any carpentering!"

"It didn't really hurt very much," Freddie replied bravely. "Is our outrigger finished?"

"Yes, I think so," Mr. Carson replied. "If you and Bert want to try it, I'll go in the office and have a chat with your father."

The scientist strolled off, while Bert and Freddie launched the canoe onto the lake. Freddie took his seat in the bow, while Bert handled the stern paddle. They pushed off from the dock and soon were gliding over the water.

"Isn't this great?" Freddie turned around to grin at Bert. "Watch!" The little boy put his hands on the sides of the canoe and swayed from side to side. "See, it won't tip over!"

"Pretty keen!" Bert agreed. "We should have done this before, and we wouldn't have landed in the lake so often!"

Freddie giggled. At this moment another canoe glided into view from around a point of land. In it were Danny Rugg and Jack Westley.

When Danny saw the Bobbsey canoe he fell back off the seat, pretending to be overcome. "Now what could that strange object be, Jack?" he called in a high, mocking voice.

"It looks like a space canoe!" Jack replied, falling in with Danny's joke.

Freddie rose to the bait. "You needn't act so smart," he cried. "This canoe won't tip over the way yours will. It's a Hawaiian outrigger!"

"You don't say!" Danny remarked in a tone of fake astonishment. "We'll see about that!"

"Don't pay any attention to them," Bert advised Freddie, swinging his canoe away from the other one.

As the Bobbseys paddled off, two pairs of hands suddenly appeared from under the water and grasped the side of their craft. The outrigger was quickly lifted off. Then the canoe was pulled over. Bert and Freddie were dumped into the water!

"Grab the paddles, Freddie!" Bert spluttered. "I'll get the outrigger!"

Both Bert and Freddie were expert swimmers. Bert quickly righted his canoe, attached the outrigger, and climbed in. Then he pulled Freddie up beside him. They were just in time to see Danny and Jack, dripping wet, paddling off at full speed. They rounded a point of land and were soon out of sight.

"How did they get over here without our seeing them?" Freddie wondered.

"When we turned our backs, they jumped in and swam over here under water," Bert surmised. "It was a typical Danny trick. I suppose he's trying to get even with us for accusing him of taking Lani's treasure."

When the boys reached the lumberyard dock, their father and Mr. Carson were waiting for them. "What in the world happened to you?" Mr. Bobbsey asked, seeing his sons' dripping clothes.

They explained the trick that Danny had played on them. "But the outrigger works fine, Mr. Carson," Freddie concluded.

The two men laughed, then the scientist said, "Just the same I think I'd better take you home so you can get into some dry clothes."

At lunch Bert and Freddie entertained the girls and Mrs. Bobbsey and Mrs. Carson with their account of the morning's adventure. Later the five children went out into the back yard to play badminton. As Flossie was running forward to hit the shuttlecock, she suddenly stopped short.

The Bobbseys' big white dog, Snap, who had been napping at the side of the lawn, was on his feet. Head down and growling, he was advancing slowly toward a row of high bushes at the rear of the yard.

"What's the matter with Snap?" Lani asked, surprised.

"Ssh! I think he hears someone back of the bushes," Flossie explained. "Snap's a very good watchdog—just like our Waggo."

The game stopped while the children watched the dog. Snap had almost reached the line of shrubbery when a stick appeared over the top of the bushes.

"Something's tied to the end of it," Nan exclaimed. As she ran forward to get the stick, Snap dashed through the hedge, barking wildly.

"It's a note!" Nan announced, returning to the group with a piece of white paper in her hand.

"What does it say? Quick!" Flossie cried impatiently.

Nan opened the paper and read:

If you want the Pele stone leave one hundred dollars under bench by fountain in park tonight.

"Oh, what will I do?" Lani cried in despair. "I don't have a hundred dollars!"

"Give me the note, Nan," Bert said. "I'll call Captain Roscoe and ask him what to do."

The other children followed Bert into the house and waited while he made the call. In a few minutes he joined them in the living room.

"What did Captain Roscoe say?" Lani asked breathlessly.

"He suggested that we make up a dummy package of money and put it under the bench. One of his officers will be in the park watching and will arrest the thief when he picks up the bundle."

"How 'citing!" Flossie cried. "May we all go along?"

"We'll have to ask Mother and Dad," Nan cautioned. "They'll be home pretty soon."

Later, when the scheme was outlined to Mr. and Mrs. Bobbsey, it was decided that only Bert and Nan should take the package to the park and that the capture of the thief would be left to the police.

The children were excited at the prospect of Lani's good luck treasure being returned, and the conversation at dinner was all about the expected capture. Bert was describing the fake package of money which he had made up when Dinah came in to say that Mr. Carson was wanted on the telephone. "It's about a telegram, sir," she explained.

When Mr. Carson returned to the dining room there was a worried look on his face. "What is it, Frank?" Mrs. Carson asked anxiously.

"It was a message from the Hawaiian Observatory," her husband replied. "It looks as if the volcano is about to erupt and they are calling all scientists back to the Park. We'll have to go home right away."

"Oh no!" Nan burst out. "Lani can't leave until we find her Pele stone!"

"Please let Lani stay here!" the other children pleaded.

Mrs. Carson looked thoughtful, then she said to Mr. and Mrs. Bobbsey with a twinkle in her eyes:

"Lani may stay if the Bobbsey family will come to Hawaii and bring her back!"

CHAPTER III

THE OLD TRUNK

AT the suggestion that they go to Hawaii, all the Bobbsey twins talked at once.

"Oh please, Mother and Dad, may we?"

"That would be perfect!"

"When can we start?"

Mr. Bobbsey held up his hand laughingly. "Just a minute, children," he said. "Your mother and I will have to talk this over. It's a long way to Hawaii, you know, and I'm not sure we can make the trip."

Then he turned to Mr. Carson. "When will you have to leave, Frank?"

The scientist said he felt that he and Mrs. Carson would have to take a plane the next afternoon. "I should get back to the island as soon as possible in view of these developments," he added.

"Then Mary and I will discuss the matter tonight and let you know tomorrow," Mr. Bobbsey said, and the children had to be content with that promise.

Later that evening two plainclothesmen, Officers Kelly and O'Brien, stopped at the Bobbsey house. "So you're working on another mystery!" Officer Kelly teased Bert. "We're to drive you to the park. Do you have the fake money ready?"

With a grin Bert showed him a package of play bills from a game he had. "These will look real enough in the dark, won't they?" he asked.

"Sure they will," Officer O'Brien agreed. "They'd almost fool me now!"

Officer Kelly drove a plain gray car to a little-used park road. Then the policemen concealed themselves behind some bushes near the fountain while Bert and Nan walked over to the bench. Quickly Bert stooped and placed the small package on the ground at one end of the seat. Then he and Nan tiptoed back and took their places with the hidden men.

They had been there only a few minutes when Nan poked Bert and pointed. A shadowy figure was approaching the bench!

"Ssh!" Officer Kelly cautioned. "Wait until he picks up the money."

The figure bent over, then straightened. "Put up your hands!" Officer O'Brien called, stepping from behind the bushes and shining his flashlight on the intruder.

"Danny Rugg!" Bert shouted.

Danny stood openmouthed in the glare of the light, a frightened look on his face. "Wh-wh-what's the matter?" he stuttered finally.

"Do you know this boy?" Officer Kelly asked.

"Sure. He's Danny Rugg and he's always trying to play tricks on us," was Bert's reply.

"You'll have to come along to headquarters with us, young man," the officer said sternly, grasping Danny by the arm.

The boy backed away. "Honest, I haven't done anything," he protested.

"It looks as if you've been trying a little extortion racket," O'Brien spoke up.

"Wh-what do you mean?" Danny quavered. "I just saw the Bobbseys get in a car with you so I followed on my bike to find out what was up."

"How about that package you have in your hand? How did you know about that?" the plain-clothesman persisted.

Danny explained that when he had lost track of the gray car he had started home across the park. Then he had seen Bert creep out from the bushes and put the package on the ground. "I just wanted to see what it was," he ended lamely.

"You mean you didn't write that note telling us to put money here so we could get Lani's Pele stone back?" Nan questioned him.

"I told you I don't know anything about that old stone, and I didn't write any note either!" Danny sputtered defiantly.

"We'll let you go this time," Officer Kelly said sternly. "But remember, boys who are always playing tricks on people, eventually get in trouble themselves."

With a muttered apology, Danny pulled his bicycle from behind a tree where he had left it and rode away.

"Well!" Bert exclaimed. "What do we do now?"

Officer O'Brien handed back the roll of fake bills which he had taken from Danny. "I'm afraid the real thief won't show up after this," he said. "If he did come and overheard all this commotion, I'm sure he's far away from here by now!"

Bert and Nan sadly agreed with the police and reported this later to the Carsons and Bobbseys who were waiting anxiously at home. "Don't be too discouraged," Mrs. Bobbsey said comfortingly. "I'm sure you'll hear from the real thief again!"

In spite of this encouragement, the children felt sad as they went upstairs to bed. This feeling was quickly changed the next morning, however, when Mr. Bobbsey announced at the breakfast table that the family would go to Hawaii!

"Oh Daddy, how scrumptious!" Flossie cried, hugging him, and Freddie did a little jig around the table.

"I'm so glad, Mary!" Mrs. Carson exclaimed.

"Frank and I are leaving this afternoon. Lani can come later with you, and I'll meet you all in Honolulu. I think you should see that city before you come to our island of Hawaii."

"I hope we can get Lani's treasure back before we leave Lakeport," Nan remarked, smiling at the little Hawaiian girl.

"Oh, I do hope so!" Lani sighed. "You're very nice to worry about it. Pele's stone really means a lot to me."

That afternoon Mr. Bobbsey drove Mr. and Mrs. Carson to the airport where they would get a plane to New York on their way back to the Hawaiian Islands. The children went along to say good-by.

When the plane was air-borne, they started back to the car. At that moment a pretty blond girl of Nan's age came up to them.

"Hello, Bobbseys!" she called. "What are you doing out here?"

"Nellie Parks!" Nan cried. "I want you to meet our friend Lani. She lives with Mother's friends the Carsons in Hawaii and we've just seen them off on their way home."

As Nellie gave the Hawaiian girl a friendly smile, Flossie spoke up. "And we're going to take Lani back to Hawaii ourselves! Isn't that 'citing?"

"You're going to Hawaii?" Nellie exclaimed. "How wonderful!" Then she gave a little laugh.

"We have an old trunk in our attic that came from there. It's full of things. Would you like to see it?"

"Is there anything special in it?" Freddie asked.

Nellie explained that the trunk, a small leather one, had belonged to her great-great-grandfather and contained some souvenirs of his. "Maybe you can all come over tomorrow morning and see the things," she suggested.

It was agreed that they would do this and the children said good-by to Nellie. The next morning when their tasks around the house had been taken care of, the five children went to the Parks' home.

Nellie was waiting for them. "Come on up to the attic," she invited.

They followed her up the stairs and into the large room. Among the modern luggage and storage boxes, they spotted the old-fashioned leather trunk.

"My great-great-grandfather's name was Silas Phinney," Nellie explained. "He was captain of a sailing ship and the trunk was made to slide under the bunk on the ship."

"When was he in Hawaii?" Lani asked with interest. "Perhaps he knew some of my ancestors."

"He probably did," Nellie said. "Anyway he sailed around the world many times and often stopped at the Hawaiian Islands. Mother says all the things in the trunk are from there."

"Let's see them," Freddie said, growing impatient with the delay.

Nellie raised the lid. The tray of the trunk was packed with small objects. Freddie spotted something interesting at once and lifted it out.

"Look at this!" he cried, holding up a little outrigger canoe. It had been carved from a small piece of teakwood. The tiny outrigger itself was made of bamboo.

"And this!" Flossie echoed. She had found a hatband fashioned of tiny yellow feathers.

"Umum." Nan sighed as she opened a sandalwood box. "Doesn't this smell heavenly?"

"There are some clothes under the tray," Nellie said. "Let's dress up like Hawaiians."

Bert lifted the tray out and set it on the floor while the girls reached into the trunk.

"What is this?" Nan giggled as she held up a long, shapeless garment of cotton.

"That's a muumuu," Lani explained. "The wives of missionaries who came to Hawaii taught our women to make those dresses. They are still popular in the islands."

"What kind of material is this, Lani?" Nellie asked. She picked up a piece of brown-and-white printed cloth.

"That's tapa. It's made from the bark of mulberry trees. We use it a great deal."

"I'd like to have a dress made from a tree!" Flossie cried, her blue eyes dancing with merriment.

"So you could 'bark' like Snap and Waggo?" Bert punned.

In the meantime Nan had put on one of the muumuus. "How do you like it?" she asked.

Lani looked critically at the dress which trailed on the floor. "It's too long, Nan. You need a girl's length. I often wear them at home. They're nice and cool."

"Aren't there any boys' clothes in there?" Freddie wanted to know.

"Oh, yes. Here's a coat for you." Nellie tossed a worn, black jacket toward the little boy.

Eagerly Freddie pulled on the coat and began to strut around the room. He thrust his hands deep into the side pockets.

"Oh, oh, there's a hole in one of these," the young twin observed. As he said this, a paper fluttered to the floor.

Bert picked it up. "It must have fallen from the coat," he said in a puzzled tone. "Let's see it, Freddie."

Together the boys examined the lining of the jacket. There was a long slit where the silk had rotted. The paper had evidently slipped through the hole in the pocket and then out the slit in the lining.

"What is it, Bert?" Nan asked.

Bert opened the yellowed paper, then passed it to Nellie. "I think it's a letter. Do you want to read it?"

Nellie took the letter. "It's funny writing," she remarked. "And listen to this!" Then she began to read.

CHAPTER IV

BERT'S PIG FRAME

THE children's eyes grew large with interest as Nellie read the letter.

"Dear Wife," it began. *"We have just made port at San Francisco after a rough voyage over the Pacific. However, this was nothing compared to the troubles we encountered in the Hawaiian Islands."*

"The letter must have been written to your great-great-grandmother by Captain Phinney," Nan exclaimed to Nellie.

"Yes," Nellie agreed, "but it was in *his* pocket. Do you suppose it was never mailed?"

"That's a good guess," Bert remarked, "but go on."

Nellie continued, *"I had determined to stop there to take on fresh food and water. But as we neared the large island of Hawaii a storm came up which blew us aground on the eastern side near the Cave of Refuge."*

"Oh, I know that cave!" Lani exclaimed in surprise. "It's not far from where the Carsons live."

"What happened next?" Flossie cried breathlessly.

Nellie turned again to the yellowed pages. *"Fearful that the jade figures which I had secured in China for the children would be lost, I buried them at the foot of a tree near the rock which the natives call 'Sitting Camel.' When the next tide came in I found my ship miraculously afloat again. In the confusion of loading her, I confess I forgot the precious jade."*

"Oh, how terrible!" Flossie exclaimed, her eyes widening in dismay.

"There's more," Nellie cautioned and went on with her reading: *"However, dear wife, I shall return for the figures on my next voyage so tell our children they will have their toys from China. Your affectionate husband, Silas Phinney."*

"How sweet!" Nan said. "Do you suppose he ever found the jade figures again?"

"Have you seen them, Nellie?" Flossie asked.

"I've never even heard about them," Nellie replied. "Let's go downstairs and ask Mother."

Quickly Nan removed the muumuu, and Freddie the coat. With Nellie clutching the old letter, the children trooped into the living room where Mrs. Parks sat reading.

Excitedly Nellie showed her the captain's letter and explained how it had fallen out of the old jacket.

When Mrs. Parks had finished reading the letter, she put it down with a puzzled look on her face. "I've never been told about the jade figures," she said, "but I seem to remember hearing that Captain Phinney died suddenly while far away from home."

She looked thoughtful while the children waited expectantly. Then she smiled. "Maybe our old family Bible will solve the mystery," she said. "It's on the lowest one of the book shelves, Nellie."

Her daughter ran over to the shelves and in a moment returned carrying a large volume. The cover was worn and brown with age. Mrs. Parks put the book on a table and the children gathered around while she opened it.

"Here it is!" she cried as she found the yellowed pages on which were recorded births, marriages, and deaths. "It's the second entry." Carefully deciphering the spidery old writing, she read:

"April 25, 1880—Silas Phinney died suddenly in San Francisco, California."

Bert hastily consulted the letter again. "This is dated April 25, 1880!" he exclaimed.

"How sad!" Nan sighed. "Captain Phinney must have written the letter just before he died, put it into his jacket, and never had a chance to mail it!"

"Then the little jade toys are still buried in Hawaii!" Freddie pointed out to the others.

"If this Cave of Refuge is near where you're going to visit," Nellie suggested, "maybe you can find them."

"Hooray!" Freddie shouted. "Now we have two mysteries to solve!"

When Nellie wanted to know what the other mystery was, the twins took turns telling her about the mysterious disappearance of Lani's treasure and how Bert and Nan had caught Danny Rugg in the park.

"I hope those officers scared Danny good and proper," Nellie said. "He's tried to trick all of us too often."

Later, at the luncheon table, Mrs. Bobbsey had a suggestion. "Wouldn't you children like to have a little party for Lani before we go away?" she asked.

The twins agreed that this would be fun. "Let's have a Hawaiian party," Flossie proposed.

"What's a Hawaiian party?" Freddie asked.

"In a book on Hawaii that we have at school," Nan remarked, "it tells about a native feast called a *luau*. Do you know what that is, Lani?"

"Yes, of course," the Polynesian girl replied. "We have *luaus* to welcome friends and on all other special occasions. They're lots of fun."

"What do you serve?" Mrs. Bobbsey asked.

Lani smiled. "The principal dish is a whole pig roasted in a pit in the ground."

"Gracious!" Mrs. Bobbsey exclaimed. "I'm afraid we can't do that!"

The children looked downcast for a moment, then Flossie brightened. "Why can't we use sausages? Aren't they part of a pig?"

Bert and Nan laughed. "At least they're *made* from a pig, honey," Nan said.

And Bert added, "I think your idea's very good, Flossie. We can make the sausages look like a pig."

"How?"

"In our shop class at school we learned to make wire shapes. If Freddie will help me, I can make a pig out of wire and we can cover it with sausages."

"That's a wonderful idea, Bert," Nan complimented him. "What's the next most important thing at a *luau,* Lani?"

"Poi."

At that moment Dinah brought in the dessert of creamy chocolate pudding. *"Poi?* What kind of groceries is that, child?" she asked.

Lani explained that *poi* was a food which the Polynesians had eaten for many years. It was a sticky, paste-like porridge made from the root of the taro plant.

"I never heard of that taro," Dinah said, "but

poi sounds sort of like cornmeal mush. Maybe that will do for your party."

Lani and the Bobbseys discussed the menu for the *luau* with Dinah, then the twins ran off to telephone their friends. It had been decided to have the party the next afternoon, and each twin was to invite one friend.

Nan called Nellie Parks, who accepted eagerly. "I want to be as much like a Hawaiian as I can," she explained, "since I have a treasure buried there."

Bert asked his best friend, Charlie Mason, while Flossie and Freddie invited their playmates, Susie Larker and Teddy Blake. All promised to be on time for the feast.

Early the next morning preparations began. While Nan, Flossie, and Lani went marketing, Bert and Freddie dug a hole at the end of the yard. A policeman stopped by to tell them the person who had demanded the money for the return of the Pele stone had not been caught.

"We're afraid he has left town," the officer said. "But we'll keep looking for him."

"Lani will hate to lose her treasure for good," Bert said.

"Yes, I know," the man said as he walked off.

The boys went on with their digging. "We'll make a bed of sticks in the bottom," Bert explained to his little brother, "then put stones on top of them. When the sticks burn, the stones will be heated. We'll put the sausage pig on the stones and cook it that way. Lani says they do it like this for a real *luau*."

Freddie ran around the yard gathering up stray sticks. Waggo, who had been frisking about, decided Freddie was playing a game with him. Each time the little boy put a stick in the hole, Waggo would grab it in his mouth and run away, with Freddie in pursuit.

Finally Freddie grew tired. He planted his feet far apart and put his fists on his hips. "Waggo," he called, "you're a bad dog! You bring those sticks right back to me!"

At the tone of Freddie's voice, Waggo stopped his romping. With his ears pricked up, his tail wagging, and still holding the sticks in his mouth, he trotted over to the hole and dropped them in!

Bert laughed. "Good boy! Now you're really helping!" He went off to fashion the wire pig frame.

The girls returned from the market, their arms full. While Freddie got the pit ready, Nan and Flossie, with Lani's help, fixed the "table" under a big tree. Lani explained that people at *luaus* always sat either on the ground or on low cushions around the feast. The ground was covered with long tapa mats on which the broad green leaves of the ti plant were spread.

"We'll have to use our regular picnic cloth in

Nan, Flossie, and Lani fixed the "table" under
a big tree

place of the tapa mat," Nan said, "but we could lay big green leaves on top of it."

Meanwhile, in the kitchen, Dinah was busy preparing the food. She had strung the link sausages on the wire frame, and it was now ready to be placed in the pit.

Next she turned to the task of making a dish of salmon, tomatoes, and onions which Lani had described to her. She had opened the cans of salmon and was beginning to peel the tomatoes when the Bobbsey's black cat Snoop walked into the room.

"Now, Snoop, you get out of here!" Dinah cried.

But she was too late. The aroma of the salmon had already reached Snoop's nostrils. With a graceful leap he landed on the counter. The cook shook her apron at the cat as he advanced on the salmon cans. At the flick of the cloth Snoop darted back, knocking into an open box of cornmeal.

Swish! The box fell over and its contents poured out onto the kitchen floor!

"You Snoop!" Dinah cried, grabbing for the animal. But Snoop was too quick for her. He leaped down from the counter and streaked out the back door, just as Bert came in.

"What in the world is the matter with Snoop?" Bert asked, laughing. "I never saw him move so fast."

"He'd *better* move fast!" Dinah muttered as she began to sweep up the cornmeal. "If I just get my hands on him . . . !"

"It's all right, Dinah," Bert said soothingly. "I'll sweep up this mess."

Pacified, Dinah returned to her cooking, and soon everything was ready for the *luau.*

The children decided that since the feast was to be spread on the ground, the dogs should be put in the kennel near the garage and Snoop in the cellar.

As the guests began to arrive, Mrs. Bobbsey produced a surprise. In a shop in Lakeport she had found some long necklaces of paper flowers which she now brought out.

"Leis!" Lani exclaimed. "Please let me present them in the Hawaiian way!"

So, as each guest arrived in the yard, Lani placed a garland around his neck, planted a light kiss on both cheeks, and cried, *"Aloha!* That means welcome," she explained.

When all the guests were there, Bert and Freddie ran to the rear of the yard to take the sausage pig from the pit. It was brown and crusty and had a delicious aroma.

Bert had just lifted the frame from the hole with a pair of tongs, when the kennel door burst open and Waggo raced out. He dashed across the lawn, grabbed the sausage pig in his teeth, and raced off!

CHAPTER V

THE BULLY'S CLUE

"STOP! Waggo, Stop!" the children screamed as the little dog ran away with the wire frame in his mouth.

But they did not have to tell him. The sausages and the frame were so hot he dropped them in a hurry and began to yelp.

"I guess it burned his mouth, poor thing," Nan said sympathetically. She went up to the dancing, prancing dog as he ran first one side of his head, then the other along the grass to ease the pain.

"I'll get some salve to put on your mouth," Nan told him.

Five minutes later Waggo felt better but went into the kennel to lie down. Freddie fastened the gate. Bert meanwhile had picked up the frame of sausages with the tongs. Much of the meat had fallen off and was now dirty.

"Oh, what'll we do?" Flossie wailed.

Dinah, who had heard the commotion and come out to investigate, chuckled as she took the wire frame from Bert. "That Waggo, he won't want sausage for a long time!" she said. "Don't you worry, Dinah's got plenty more sausages cooked right in this kitchen. You all sit down and I'll bring them out."

As the children arranged themselves around the leaf-and-flower-covered picnic cloth, Nan whispered to Bert, "How do you suppose Waggo got out of the kennel? The gate was fastened."

Little Teddy Blake, who was seated next to Nan, overhead the question. "I saw Danny Rugg sneaking around the corner of the garage just as Waggo ran out," he piped up. "Maybe he unlocked the gate."

"That's the answer then!" Bert exclaimed. "Our friend Danny again!"

"Well, let's enjoy the *luau*," Lani urged.

There was a green paper plate and half a coconut shell filled with white cornmeal mush for each person.

"This is *poi*," Flossie explained to the guests as she saw their puzzled looks. "It may taste like mush but you must pretend it's Hawaiian *poi*. All the Polynesians eat it!"

Dinah arrived with a platter of crispy brown sausages and baked sweet potatoes. Nan jumped up to help. At each place she put down a small saucer of the salmon and tomato preparation.

"Say, this looks great!" Charlie Mason remarked as he opened his gaily flowered paper napkin.

Just then Mrs. Bobbsey came into the yard followed by a young man carrying a camera.

"Children," she said, smiling, "this is Mr. Thomas. He has come to take your picture for the *Lakeport Times.*"

Susie Larker squealed in excitement. "Oh, won't my mother be surprised when she sees my picture in the paper!"

The boys and girls rearranged their leis and turned smiling faces to the camera. After the young man had taken several shots, he made a list of all the children's names and addresses.

When he wrote down Lani's name, Flossie explained that the dark-eyed girl was from Hawaii. "We're going to take her home!" she announced importantly.

"All the way to Hawaii?" Mr. Thomas asked in surprise.

"Yes," Freddie spoke up. "We're going to fly to San Francisco and stay there awhile, and then we're going to Honolulu on another plane!"

"That's wonderful," the young man said. "I hope you'll all have a good time." Then he shook hands with Mrs. Bobbsey, thanked her, and left.

When the children had finished their feast, topped off by a dessert of coconut pudding, Nan suggested that Lani dance a hula for them. "We

The young man took several shots

have a record of Hawaiian music. I'll put the player on the back porch and you'll be able to hear it."

While this was being done, Lani ran into the house and returned wearing a white blouse and a skirt made of broad green ti leaves.

"Oh Lani, you look bee-yoo-ti-ful!" Flossie exclaimed.

As the plaintive Hawaiian melody began on the record player, Lani explained that each hula told a story, sometimes sad, sometimes romantic, and sometimes even funny.

"The movement of the hands is the most important part of the dance," she said. "Fluttering fingers mean falling rain. A wide sweep of the arms pictures wind, swaying palm trees, or birds flying. And this means leaping porpoises."

The children laughed, as Lani's arms and fingers imitated the playful animals jumping in and out of the water. When the dance ended, everyone applauded enthusiastically.

"I wish I could go to Hawaii too," Nellie sighed wistfully.

"Never mind," Nan comforted her, "we'll bring back the Chinese jade figures for you."

Later, after the young guests had all left, Mr. Bobbsey showed the twins the tickets which he had purchased that day. "We'll leave here the day after tomorrow," he announced.

"Hurrah!" shouted Freddie.

The next morning Mrs. Bobbsey asked Bert and Nan to go downtown and do some last minute shopping for her. They were walking along the street when Nan suddenly clutched Bert's arm. "Look!" she cried. "There's Danny Rugg! What'll we say to let him know we found out the trick he played?"

"Let's fool him," Bert proposed. "Don't mention the luau or what happened when Waggo got out of the kennel. But I do want to ask him something else."

Nan agreed that silence would probably annoy Danny more than if they complained. As they reached the bully, Bert called, "Hi, Danny. I'd like to ask you a question."

"What is it?"

"You remember the other day when we saw you in the Soda Shop with Jack Westley?"

Danny grudgingly acknowledged that he did.

"I looked back and saw that man with the dark glasses talking to you. What was he saying?"

"It's none of your business," Danny replied defiantly, "but he wanted to know who those crazy kids were who believed in volcano goddesses!"

"Did you tell him?"

"Sure. Why not?" With that the bully resumed his amble down the street.

Nan turned to Bert, her eyes shining with excitement. "I'm positive that man is the one who stole Lani's treasure!" she cried. "He heard us talking about the Pele stone. Then he found out who we were and came to the house that night and stole Lani's treasure!"

"You could be right, Nan," Bert agreed. "Let's stop at police headquarters and tell Captain Roscoe about the man."

The police officer was at his desk when the twins reached the station. He listened carefully to their story. "Give me a description of this fellow," he said finally, drawing a pad toward him. "I'll have my men check the motels and rooming houses."

Nan described the stranger while Captain Roscoe made notes. "Very good," the officer said. "We'll start on this right away and let you know the results."

When Bert and Nan told him that they were leaving the next day, the captain took their addresses in San Francisco and Hawaii and promised to notify them if he found the man they suspected.

Arriving home, Bert and Nan found everyone busy with preparations for the trip. Flossie had laid all her dolls on the bed.

"I just can't decide which children to take," she announced importantly when her older brother and sister came into her room. "But I think maybe Jean and Linda would enjoy the trip most."

At this moment Freddie ran in, his arms laden

with a toy fire engine, a toy pumper, and a red fire helmet. "I can't get these in my suitcase, Flossie. Can you put them in yours?"

"Of course not, silly!" his twin replied. "Ask Mother to put them in hers. It's bigger."

In a few minutes Freddie returned, followed by Mrs. Bobbsey. "You know, children," she explained, "we're flying and have to be careful not to take too much heavy luggage. I think this time Freddie and Flossie will have to take only one toy apiece—and small ones at that."

Noticing the disappointed looks on the faces of the younger twins, she said consolingly, "I'm sure there will be so much to do in Hawaii that you won't have time to play with toys."

Flossie brightened. "That's right. Let's leave them all at home, Freddie. I will if you will!"

Freddie agreed reluctantly. "I might need my pumper with all those volcanoes around," he said, "but I'll leave it here."

With this problem settled, the packing was soon completed and the luggage carried downstairs ready for the next day's journey. Very early in the morning, Sam drove the group to the local airport, and they boarded the plane for New York City. A few hours later they arrived at the big New York airport from which the long-distance jet planes left.

"Ooh!" Flossie exclaimed as she saw the large, silvery craft. "Isn't it huge?"

"First stop, San Francisco!" Mr. Bobbsey called as he shepherded the children aboard.

They all settled into the comfortable seats and fastened their seat belts. In a few minutes the big plane began to taxi out for the take-off.

The twins and Lani grinned at one another. "We're really off to Hawaii!" Nan exclaimed.

Just then the plane stopped and a voice came over the loud-speaker. "Ladies and gentlemen, this is the captain. We are returning to the airport!"

CHAPTER VI

A SURPRISE MESSAGE

RETURNING to the airport! The passengers in the plane murmured uneasily. What could be wrong? In a few minutes the huge craft stopped at the departure building again. Once more the voice came over the loud-speaker:

"We are going to make slight repairs. You may leave the plane if you wish, but we will take off in approximately one hour."

"Would you like to get out, children?" Mrs. Bobbsey asked.

"Yes, let's," Nan spoke up. "We can go in the waiting room and look around."

They all trooped from the plane and into the building. Freddie and Flossie noticed a toy shop and ran in that direction. Mr. and Mrs. Bobbsey and the older children paused at a book-and-stationery counter.

Suddenly Flossie came running back. "Lani," she cried breathlessly, "your Pele stone is in the window of the shop over here!"

"Oh, I want to see!" Lani exclaimed. She and the older twins followed Flossie as the little girl darted away through the crowd.

When they caught up with Flossie, she and Freddie were standing by a shop window filled with Oriental vases and carved ornaments of all kinds. At the very back of the display was an oddly shaped piece of reddish stone.

"It does look like yours, Lani," Nan remarked, opening the door of the shop and going in.

A pleasant-looking Japanese woman came to wait on her. At Nan's request the woman took the ornament from the window. By this time Lani was standing beside her friend.

"Oh no, that isn't my stone," the Hawaiian girl sighed in disappointment.

The children took turns telling the friendly clerk about the theft of the Polynesian relic. The woman was very sympathetic. "I am so sorry," she said. "But I feel sure you will find your stone. Such things always return to their rightful owners."

Lani and the Bobbseys thanked the kindly Japanese clerk and resumed their tour of the waiting room. After a while Mr. Bobbsey called to them that the plane was ready to leave. This time the take-off was uneventful and soon the great craft was flying high over the green countryside.

It was late afternoon when the jet set down at the busy San Francisco airport. As soon as the steps were in place and the door opened, the passengers began to disembark. Bert and Freddie were among the last to leave the plane.

Just as the brothers reached the ground, an airline attendant came running up to them. "Was the Bobbsey family on this flight?" he called to the pretty stewardess who stood at the top of the steps.

"I'm Bert Bobbsey," Bert spoke up.

The man whirled around, a relieved expression on his face. "Whew!" he exclaimed. "I was afraid I'd missed you. A letter for the Bobbsey Twins."

Bert took the proffered envelope and re-marked with a grin, "Well, I'm one of the twins, but I don't know who sent the letter."

"Maybe it's the Lakeport police," Freddie suggested. "I'll bet they've found the thief."

Bert thanked the messenger, then took Freddie's arm. "We'd better catch up to Mother and Dad, or they'll think we're lost!"

A few minutes later the two boys found the rest of the group waiting for the luggage to be brought from the plane. Bert explained the boys' delay and held up the letter.

"Read it, Bert!" Flossie cried impatiently.

Quickly he tore open the envelope. Inside was a typewritten note. "Wow! Listen to this," Bert exclaimed.

The letter was unsigned and directed the Bobbseys to take money to the Golden Lotus Restaurant in San Francisco's Chinatown the next evening. They would then be given information as to where to pick up the missing Pele stone.

"It's here!" Lani exclaimed. "My precious Pele stone is in San Francisco. How wonderful!"

Mr. Bobbsey loked doubtful. "Don't be too hopeful, Lani," he cautioned. "I don't understand this at all. How could the stone, stolen in Lakeport, turn up so soon in San Francisco? And how did the thief know we would be here?"

"I agree, Richard," Mrs. Bobbsey remarked.

"Perhaps you should report the whole matter to the police."

"You're right, Mary. I'll call them the moment we reach the hotel."

An hour later, when they were settled in a large suite at a downtown hotel, Mr. Bobbsey put in the call. "I'll send Lieutenant Pratt over to see you at once," the police chief promised.

In a short time there was a knock on the door and Bert admitted a tall, blond man with penetrating blue eyes. He introduced himself as Lieutenant Pratt. After taking out his notebook, the officer began to make some entries as Lani told the story of her Polynesian treasure and its disappearance. Then Bert showed Lieutenant Pratt the letter which had been delivered to them at the airport.

"Hmm," the officer said thoughtfully. "I'll take this and see what the boys in the lab can make of it. Then I think the best thing for you people to do is to go to the Golden Lotus tomorrow night and see what happens. I'll be there, too, keeping an eye on things."

"Goody," Flossie said. "I'm glad we're going to Chinatown. I want to see some little Chinese boys and girls."

The officer smiled. "You'll see lots of them there." Then he turned to Mr. Bobbsey. "You'll also get a delicious dinner at the Golden Lotus. They specialize in Peking duck."

"That sounds dreamy," said Nan. "I can hardly wait."

Mr. Bobbsey escorted the officer to the door. "Thank you, Lieutenant," he said as they shook hands. "We'll count on seeing you tomorrow night."

As Flossie sleepily prepared for bed a little later, she marveled, "Just think, last night I went to bed in Lakeport. This morning I was in New York, and now I'm in San Francisco."

"And the day after tomorrow you'll be in Hawaii," Lani reminded her with a happy smile.

The next morning Mr. Bobbsey announced that he had hired a large car with a driver to show them the city. When it arrived, they found the driver to be a jolly-looking man of middle age.

"Just call me Tim," he urged as they drove off.

"Where are we going first, Tim?" Freddie asked. He sat in front between his father and the chauffeur.

"I'm going to take you to one of the most beautiful parks in the world," Tim said proudly. "It's called the Golden Gate Park. You know San Francisco Harbor is called the Golden Gate, and the park has the same name."

"I'd like to see the Japanese Garden there," Mrs. Bobbsey called from the back seat. "I've heard so much about it."

"We'll stop there first, ma'am," Tim agreed.

In a short while he stopped the car near the park entrance, then jumped out and opened the doors. "You'll all want to take a walk through the garden. I'll wait here."

The Bobbseys strolled along together, admiring the beautiful spot.

"Oh. See those little trees!" Flossie pointed to plantings of low, spreading trees.

Nan nodded. "They're such pretty shapes, too."

The children were fascinated by the rocks of varying sizes placed artistically about.

Presently Bert stopped to examine a huge lantern carved in stone. Meanwhile, Nan, Flossie, and Lani ran up a path to watch a young man taking a picture of a Japanese girl in a bright-flowered kimono.

Freddie lingered behind, pausing occasionally to pick up a pebble from the path. The little boy did not notice where he was going. Suddenly he looked up and stared in surprise. Right in front of him was the strangest bridge he had ever seen. It seemed to go almost straight up and then down again.

"It's like an upside-down U," he exclaimed to himself.

The bridge was so steep that cleats had been nailed across the floor to help people walk over it.

"It sure would be fun to slide down that railing!" thought Freddie.

Impulsively, clinging to the railing and placing his feet on the cleats, he pulled himself up to the center of the bridge.

Next, Freddie climbed up and straddled the railing. "Here I go," he cried.

With a push of his hands he started the downward slide. But the railing was so steep and slick that Freddie could not stop when he reached the bottom. Off he flew, and landed on the path at the foot of the bridge!

"Ow!" Freddie muttered. One knee had been painfully scraped by a sharp stone.

As he got up, he was startled to hear a small voice near him say:

"Ohio! Good morning!"

Freddie looked around to see a Japanese boy about his age bowing from the waist. "You have hurt yourself? Follow me—Saito—to the tea house, where we live. My mother will fix your cuts."

"Is Saito your name?" Freddie asked. "I'm Freddie Bobbsey."

He followed the kind Japanese boy into an attractive tea house nestled among the trees of the garden. A pretty woman in a dark blue kimono came to meet them. "What is it, my son?" she asked Saito.

"This is Freddie Bobbsey. He has hurt his knee."

"Oh yes, I see." The woman hurried from the

room and returned with antiseptic and bandages. In a moment Freddie's scrapes had been cleaned and neatly covered.

"Thank you very much," Freddie said politely.

Saito giggled. "In Japanese we say *dozo* to thank for something."

"*Dozo* very much," Freddie replied with a low bow.

Saito and his mother laughed. "You make a fine Japanese boy," the woman praised him.

A short while later Mr. and Mrs. Bobbsey and the other twins entered the tea house. They were amazed to find Freddie seated on the floor at a low table drinking tea with Saito and his mother.

"Freddie!" Mrs. Bobbsey exclaimed. "We've been looking everywhere for you!"

Sheepishly Freddie explained about his fall on the bridge and displayed his bandaged knee. Mrs. Bobbsey thanked Saito's mother for taking care of her son, then Freddie, his family, and Lani went back to the garden entrance where Tim awaited them.

The balance of the day was spent seeing the sights of the interesting city. All the children loved the playful seals at Seal Rocks best.

"I'd love to have one for a pet at home." Flossie's eyes danced.

"Me too," Freddie agreed. "We could have our own trained-seal act."

Mr. Bobbsey threw back his head and laughed. "No slippery seals in the house, please!"

But that evening even the amusing seals were forgotten as the Bobbseys and Lani set out for the Golden Lotus Restaurant.

"Oh, I hope we do find out where your Pele stone is," Nan said to her Hawaiian friend.

All the children were excited at the prospect of solving the mystery. Nevertheless, they also enjoyed walking along Grant Avenue, the main street of Chinatown. The shop windows were full of strange foods, brightly colored kimonos, and carved ivory ornaments.

When they entered the restaurant, the head waiter led them to a large table in one corner of the room. At a nearby table the children saw Lieutenant Pratt. He was seated with another man and gave no sign of recognition when the Bobbsey party had come in.

"I want to try the peeping duck," Flossie declared as she picked up a menu.

The waiter, who had come to take their order, smiled broadly.

"Oh, yes. The Peking duck. An excellent dish."

Everyone decided to have the duck, as well as a thin chicken soup and rice with vegetables.

Then several platters were set on the table: one of sliced onion sprouts; one of what looked like uncooked pancakes; and a third plate piled with slices of crusty duck.

"There is a special way we Chinese eat Peking duck," the waiter said.

"Please tell us," Nan urged.

"First," the waiter said, "you take one of these cakes. Then put some pieces of duck on it; next, pile on some slices of onion. Sprinkle it with soy sauce, then fold the cake like this, and eat it in your fingers."

Giggling, the children promptly began following his directions. Freddie grinned. "This is the funniest sandwich I ever made." He took a bite of the concoction. "Yum. It tastes good."

As they ate, Bert and Nan kept glancing around the room. Both twins were expecting a note or signal of some kind demanding the money for revealing the location of Lani's treasure.

To their disappointment, there was no word from the thief. The Bobbseys and Lani waited until the table had been cleared, then Mr. Bobbsey stood up.

"Well," he announced, "we might as well go back to the hotel." He looked toward Lieutenant Pratt who nodded slightly.

"What do you suppose happened?" Nan whispered as they went out.

"Something must have gone wrong," Bert declared.

When the group entered the hotel lobby, Bert went over to the mail desk and returned with an envelope. "Here's another letter," he announced excitedly. "It looks like the one we got at the airport."

"Quick, open it!" Freddie urged.

Bert did so and drew out another typed message. Everyone gasped as he read the frightening words:

KEEP POLICE OUT OF THIS OR YOU WILL NEVER RECOVER THE PELE STONE!

CHAPTER VII

CABLE CAR EXCITEMENT

"THE thief *was* at the Golden Lotus!" Nan exclaimed. "He must have recognized Lieutenant Pratt and been frightened away!"

"And we're leaving for Hawaii tomorrow!" Lani wailed. "I'll never get my treasure back!"

Mr. and Mrs. Bobbsey tried to comfort the little Hawaiian girl by assuring her that the San Francisco police would continue the search for the thief.

"And just think, Lani," Flossie added, "you'll soon be home again!"

"Even before we leave San Francisco, we can have some more fun," Bert said to cheer Lani. "Let's ride on one of those cable cars," he suggested.

Bert had been interested in watching the little cars which were pulled up and down the hilly

streets by a cable set into the ground between the tracks.

"We'll do it right after breakfast tomorrow," his father promised.

The next morning Mr. and Mrs. Bobbsey and the children climbed aboard a cable car which ran past their hotel. It was a busy time of day and the little vehicle was crowded. Freddie and

Flossie with their parents found seats in the open front section. The inside was full, so Bert, Nan, and Lani stood on the back platform.

"This is great!" Nan cried as the little car jerked its way up the steep slope. At each cross street the children caught glimpses of the sparkling blue waters of San Francisco Bay far below.

When the cable car reached the top of the high hill, it started down the other side. Faster and faster it went. Looking through the middle section, Bert could see the motorman in the front. He seemed to be having trouble with the brakes.

"Say! I don't think the brakes are holding!" Bert exclaimed. Just then he saw an old-fashioned wheel on the back platform. "I'll bet this is another brake!" he said.

Quickly Bert grasped the wheel and tugged on it. For a moment nothing happened, then as he pulled harder, the runaway car began to slow down.

Nan and Lani had been holding their breaths. Now Lani cried, "You've stopped it! Oh thank you, Bert! You saved our lives!"

Just then the conductor arrived on the back platform. "Are you the boy who put on the brake?" he asked.

When Bert nodded, the man put a hand on the boy's shoulder. "Thanks, son. The front brakes weren't taking hold properly. Of course, the car would have stopped when it reached the turn-table at the end of the line, but we might have had an accident on the way down. You used your head."

Other passengers heard him and also praised Bert. When Flossie was told what had happened she announced to those around, "My big brother is a cable-car hero."

"Indeed he is," said a woman seated nearby, and the boy's parents too felt proud of him.

When the ride was over the Bobbseys returned to the hotel with Lani. In their mailbox was a notice saying Lieutenant Pratt had telephoned.

"Maybe he has some information," Nan said excitedly. "Anyway, we should tell him about that note we received last night."

Bert agreed. He put in a call to the police officer and read him the warning message.

"I'll be right over," the officer told him. He arrived within a few minutes. "I'll keep this with the other letter," he said, putting it into his pocket. "I'm sure we can pick up this thief and I'll let you know at your address in Hawaii."

Mr. Bobbsey thanked the lieutenant, and the travelers left for the airport. There was just time to check their luggage before the plane for Honolulu was ready for boarding.

"Stay together and follow me," Mr. Bobbsey directed as he led the way down the ramp to the gate from which their plane was to leave.

The attendant took the tickets, then remarked:
"You're one person short, sir."

The children's mother looked around quickly.
"Where's Flossie?" she cried. "Have any of you
seen her?"

"Maybe she slipped through the gate ahead of
us," Bert suggested. Then he pointed across the
airstrip. "There she is!" Flossie was running toward another plane which was parked nearby.

"I'll get her," Freddie volunteered eagerly,
and darted after his twin. In a few minutes he
was back holding Flossie by the hand.

"You must stay with us, dear," Mrs. Bobbsey
said reprovingly.

"But Mommy," Flossie protested, "I saw the
Soda Shop man and I wanted to ask him if he
took Lani's Pele stone!"

"You saw him!" Bert exclaimed. "Where was
he going?"

Flossie explained that she had noticed a tanned
man with bushy black hair and dark glasses going down another ramp. She had run after him
as he walked toward a plane. "Then Freddie
came and pulled me over here!" she added indignantly. "I wanted to see if he was the bad person
we're trying to find."

"I'm sorry," said Freddie.

"Please take your seats in the aircraft," the
attendant said politely. "It's ready for take-off."

"Maybe 'Mr. Dark Glasses' is going to Hawaii too," Nan said hopefully, and asked the ticket-taker where the other plane was headed.

"I really don't know," he answered. "Please get aboard."

Sighing, the twins and Lani hurried to the plane and found their seats. Soon after the craft was air-borne, the pretty Japanese stewardess changed from her neat blue uniform into a beautiful flowered kimono. As she passed the seat where Nan and Lani were, she smiled. "Would you two girls like to help me serve the meal?" she asked.

"Oh yes!" they exclaimed.

The stewardess beckoned them to follow her. When they reached the tiny galley at the rear of the cabin she gave each girl a kimono.

Nan and Lani quickly slipped into the gay robes. Then they began to laugh. The garments dragged around their feet.

"We wear them long," the hostess explained, "but not that long!" Holding up two long sashes she said, "These are the *obis*. We'll tuck the kimonos up around your waists and then adjust the obis."

Deftly she wound the sashes and arranged the large bows in the rear. In a minute two Japanese-appearing girls stood before her!

"You look darling," the stewardess exclaimed. She gave each girl a tray piled with tightly rolled hot towels. "These are called *o-shibori*. It is a

Japanese custom to wipe the hands and face with a warm, damp towel before every meal. After each passenger has had one of these, we will serve the meal."

The passengers smiled when Nan and Lani walked down the aisle balancing their trays. The girls were even trying to copy the mincing little steps of the stewardess.

When Nan carried a tray of food to a large, blond woman who was seated behind Freddie and Flossie, the woman shook her head. "Oh dear," she cried, "I don't know how I'm going to eat anything. I have to hold this box on my lap!"

As she spoke the woman indicated a large, square cardboard container. "I'm Mrs. Rice," she said. "I'm taking a special birthday cake to my daughter who lives in Honolulu. The stewardess tells me it's against the rules to put anything like this in the overhead rack."

"I'll set your tray on top of the box," Nan said helpfully. "Can you manage that way?"

"Thank you, dear," the woman said gratefully. "I think that will work fine."

Later, when Nan and Lani had changed to their own clothes and returned to their seats, the stewardess served their meal. Flossie called across the aisle to the Hawaiian girl. "Please tell us some Hawaiian words before we get to Honolulu."

Lani giggled. "As soon as I'm *pau, malihini.*"

"What does that mean?" Bert asked.

"*Pau* is through, finished," Lani replied. "*Ma-lihini* means newcomer. I am a *kamaaina* or old-timer."

"How do you say 'thank you'?" Flossie wanted to know.

"That is *mahalo,* and *mahalo nui loa* is thank you very much."

Lani explained that the Hawaiian language had only twelve letters—five vowels and seven consonants. "That is the reason so many of the words sound alike," she added. "People in the islands mix Hawaiian words with their English, so you'll probably hear more Hawaiian ones while you're visiting there."

By this time the stewardess had removed Flossie's tray. The little girl, remembering that the woman behind her had a birthday cake, stood up on the seat and leaned over the back. "How is your package getting along?" she asked.

Mrs. Rice smiled at the curly-haired little girl with the big blue eyes. "Would you like to see the cake?" she asked.

"Oh yes!" Flossie cried. "I just love birthday cakes!"

When the lid of the box was raised, Flossie saw that the top of the cake was decorated with roses and garlands made of different colored icings. "Oh, it's bee-yoo-ti-ful!" she exclaimed.

In the meantime Freddie had finished his dinner and was trying to find the bell to summon the stewardess. "I guess this is it," he decided, feeling a button at the end of the arm rest between his seat and Flossie's.

Freddie pushed the button firmly. *Wham!* The back of Flossie's seat fell down and threw the little girl into the seat behind. She landed headfirst on the birthday cake!

CHAPTER VIII

A SURFBOARD SPILL

AS Flossie fell into the birthday cake, the woman threw up her hands in horror. "Oh dear!" she cried. "My lovely present!"

Flossie spluttered, raising her head. She was a sorry sight. Butter-cream frosting stuck to her face and dribbled down the front of her pink cotton dress. Her lower lip quivered. "I didn't mean to spoil your birthday cake," she sobbed.

At this moment Mrs. Bobbsey reached her little daughter, and the stewardess ran up the aisle. Together they helped Flossie and the woman to their feet and the stewardess carried off the ruined cake.

Mrs. Bobbsey apologized for the mishap and then took Flossie to the wash room to get clean. When they returned, Mrs. Rice had calmed down. "Accidents will happen," she said consolingly to Flossie, patting the little girl on the arm

The stewardess came up to the woman carrying a small bundle wrapped in a gaily printed piece of cloth. "I have brought you some special Japanese birthday cakes for your daughter," she said. "And I have put them in a *furoshiki*. We Japanese carry our packages in a square piece of cloth like this. We think it is easier to manage than a bag."

Mrs. Rice thanked the stewardess and said, "I'm sure my daughter will like these very much."

Some time later the stewardess looked out the window. "We are coming into Honolulu in a few minutes," she said over the loud-speaker. As she spoke, the "fasten-seat-belts" sign flashed on.

While the passengers were buckling their belts, the Japanese girl continued, "If you look out the window you will see Diamond Head. It is the famous symbol of Honolulu."

"Why is it called Diamond Head?" Bert called out.

"It is an extinct volcano, once thought to be the home of the volcano goddess, Pele. Sailors exploring the crater found some shiny crystals which they thought were diamonds, so they named the place Diamond Head."

Darkness was creeping over the island now, and the lights along the shoreline and running up the nearby mountains seemed to form a giant necklace of jewels. In a few minutes the big plane set down at the Honolulu airport.

As the Bobbsey party descended the steps from the plane, Lani ran ahead. When she saw a smiling woman at the gate, she cried out, "Aunt Jane! Here we all are!"

Mrs. Carson stepped forward and as the Bobbseys passed through the gate she put sweet-smelling leis of flowers around their necks, kissed them, and cried, *"Aloha!"*

"What a lovely welcome!" Mrs. Bobbsey exclaimed. "And what are the flowers? They're beautiful."

"Plumeria," Mrs. Carson replied. "They grow on the islands in all colors."

The luggage was soon collected and the group piled into a limousine for the trip to the hotel on Waikiki Beach where Mrs. Carson had made reservations.

"I was able to get a bungalow with four bedrooms," she explained, "so we'll all be close together."

The car pulled up before the main section of the hotel, and several smiling boys piled the luggage onto a cart. The party followed the boys through a beautiful garden and stopped before a small, one-story house.

The boys carried the luggage into the bedrooms, then one left while the other bowed and said, "I am Saikai, your room boy."

Solemnly Freddie bowed from the waist and replied, *"Ohio,* Saikai."

Mrs. Bobbsey looked at her son in amazement. "Why, Freddie!" she exclaimed. "Where did you learn that?"

"The little Japanese boy in the San Francisco park taught me," Freddie explained proudly.

Saikai was delighted and promised to take good care of them all during their stay at the beach.

The next morning the children arrived at the outdoor dining room in their bathing suits. As they sat eating breakfast they looked out at the calm blue ocean.

"See the surf-riders." Lani pointed. Far out, gracefully poised on surfboards, were four bronzed young men. As the Bobbseys watched, a long rolling wave caught the boards and propelled them at a fast pace toward the beach.

"Boy!" Bert exclaimed. "That looks keen. I'd like to learn that sport."

"Look!" Flossie cried. "One of the men has a doggie on the board with him!" Sure enough, a shaggy pup sat proudly on the front of the last surfboard. As it rode the waves, the dog managed to stick on.

When breakfast was over the children dashed to the beach. "Let's walk up a ways," Bert proposed to Nan.

They had gone only a short distance when a boy in his early teens came up to them. "You just came last night, didn't you?" he asked in a friendly manner. He was taller and slimmer than Bert and wore his blond hair in a crew cut. "My name's Arnold Cooper. What's yours?"

Bert introduced Nan and himself. "Have you been here long?" he asked their new acquaintance.

"About a week. We're going over to the island of Hawaii where the big volcanoes are in a few days." Then he went on, "Come meet Aka. He's the hotel beach boy and he'll teach you how to surfboard if you want to learn."

Aka was a muscular young man with black

hair and flashing brown eyes. When Bert and Nan expressed their interest in learning to ride the waves, he brought over two surfboards and put them into the water.

Then he showed the twins how to lie on the boards and use their arms to paddle out to where the rollers formed. "Then you turn around very carefully and stand up on the board, balancing yourself by stretching out your arms."

Arnold paddled along beside them and when Aka gave the signal, the three young people got to their feet. When the next wave reached them, Aka sped on ahead. Nan, who was between Bert and Arnold, had gained her balance.

"Isn't this wonderful!" she cried, as the board raced toward shore on the crest of the wave.

At this moment Arnold's board hit hers. Nan fell, striking her head on the edge of it.

Quickly Bert slipped off his board. "Hold on, Nan!" he cried. "I'll tow you to shore!"

Arnold had managed to retain his balance and was still speeding toward the beach. By the time Bert and Nan reached the sand, he was waiting to help them in. "Bad luck, Nan," he sympathized. "Are you all right?"

"Yes," Nan replied coolly. When Arnold left them to walk back up the beach, she turned to Bert. "I'm sure Arnold ran his board into mine deliberately."

"Are you positive?" Bert said in surprise. "He seems nice."

"Well, maybe I'm wrong," Nan replied, "but I don't think so. Somehow I don't trust him."

Bert and Nan thanked Aka for the lesson, then caught up with Arnold. They introduced the boy to Freddie and Flossie and Lani, who were playing in the sand.

When Arnold mentioned that he was leaving in a few days for the island of Hawaii, Flossie piped up, "We are too. We're going to find a treasure there!"

In spite of Nan's warning glance, Flossie told Arnold the story of the jade figures which had been buried near the Cave of Refuge on the shore of Hawaii so long ago.

Arnold looked interested, but his only comment was, "Maybe I'll see you there."

Mr. Bobbsey came on the beach while they were still discussing the treasure. "I have a surprise for you," he announced.

"Oh Daddy," Flossie cried, "I love s'prises! What is it?"

"You know those pink-and-white jeeps you were admiring last evening?"

On the way to the hotel the evening before the children had been interested in the little jeeps which they had seen on the streets. The vehicles were painted a bright pink, and had a pink-and-white-striped awning for a roof.

"Yes, they're keen!" Bert agreed.

"I've rented one to use while we're in Honolulu," Mr. Bobbsey explained. "I think I'll take a run out to the museum this morning. Would any of you like to go with me? Your mother and Mrs. Carson have gone shopping."

Freddie and Flossie decided that they would rather stay on the beach and Lani elected to remain with them. Bert, Nan, and Arnold said they would be interested in visiting the museum and ran off to dress.

"I'll meet you in the drive in front of the hotel," Mr. Bobbsey called after them.

Soon they were in the jeep and driving through the busy Honolulu streets to the museum. When they reached it, they began to stroll through the rooms.

A tall, gray-haired man came up to them and introduced himself as Mr. Grove. "I'm acting curator here while the regular man is away on an expedition," he explained. "I'll be glad to show you around. You know, we have a very famous collection of Polynesian articles."

"Look at these capes and helmets!" Nan exclaimed as she paused before a glass case. "What are they made of?"

"Feathers," was the reply. "The Polynesians fashioned many things from the feathers of the tiny iiwi and mamo birds which are now extinct. These capes were worn by the ancient kings. The one belonging to Kamehameha the Great is valued at a million dollars and is shown only on rare occasions."

"When did Kamehameha live?" Bert asked.

"Toward the end of the eighteenth, and beginning of the nineteenth, century," Mr. Grove replied. "It was he who united all these islands under one rule in 1810.

"These royal standards you see are also made of feathers," the curator went on, pointing to long poles on the tops of which were elaborate arrangements of feathers. "Some of our younger visitors think they look more like feather dusters than standards," he said with a smile. "They are called *kahili.*"

The group now entered a long exhibition room.

"What is that?" Nan asked. She looked at a huge hollowed-out log about ten feet long which rested on a sort of trestle.

"That is an ancient Samoan church gong," Mr. Grove explained. "When the chief priest wished to summon the people of the village to church, he struck the log with this club." He pointed out a long piece of wood near the gong. "It makes a deep, resounding noise when hit with this."

The group moved on to a small thatched hut on a platform in the center of the room. "We have here an exact replica of a Polynesian house," the curator said. "It—"

At that moment the twins were startled by a loud *boom!*

CHAPTER IX

A SUSPICIOUS VISITOR

AS the sound filled the room, startling all the sight-seers, an expression of annoyance came over Mr. Grove's face. "Someone is playing with the Samoan gong," he said. "We ask our visitors not to touch it."

Mr. Bobbsey had walked into the native house, but Bert and Nan followed the curator back in the direction of the gong. When they reached it, no one was nearby.

"What happened?" a voice asked. Turning, the twins saw Arnold, who had apparently just wandered in from another room.

When Mr. Grove explained, Arnold said he had not noticed anyone around the huge log. Nan looked significantly at Bert and, when Arnold walked off with the curator, she whispered:

"I think it was Arnold who struck the gong. He stayed back there when we went to look at the hut. He just pretended to be coming in from that other room."

"Maybe you're right, Nan," Bert replied in a low tone.

When they reached Mr. Bobbsey, he had left the native hut and was examining a framed chart on the wall of the exhibition hall. "Here's a pretty good record of the old Polynesian gods and goddesses," he said to the twins.

Nan pressed closer to get a good look. "There's Pele!" she exclaimed.

Mr. Grove and Arnold walked up at this moment. The curator, who had heard Nan's exclamation, spoke up. "Yes, Pele, the goddess of volcanoes, is one of the most important of the early deities. Have you heard about the time she helped Kamehameha to conquer the island of Hawaii?"

"No," Nan said. "Please tell us!"

"Kamehameha was battling Keoua, who ruled Hawaii," the curator began. "Keoua's warriors were pursuing Kamehameha's forces when they passed by Pele's home, the volcano of Kilauea. There was a great eruption and every warrior was killed, so Kamehameha won the battle!"

"Good for Pele!" Bert exclaimed.

"Speaking of the volcano goddess," Mr. Grove said, "a curious thing happened just this morning."

"What was that?" Mr. Bobbsey inquired.

"A man came in the museum to see me. He had a stone object which he wanted to sell. He claimed it was an ancient Polynesian relic sacred to Pele."

"Was it a queer reddish color?" Nan asked.

"Why, yes it was," the curator replied in surprise.

"Lani's Pele stone!" Nan cried.

The curator looked startled. "What did you say, young lady?"

Breathlessly Nan poured out the story of Lani's stolen treasure and the twins' attempt to recover it. When she had finished, Bert asked, "Did you buy the stone, sir?"

Mr. Grove shook his head. "No, I didn't. I'm always suspicious of people coming in off the street with articles of value to sell. I told the fellow that I would require some sort of evidence to prove that the stone was authentic."

"What did he say to that?" Mr. Bobbsey asked.

"He became very angry, turned on his heel, and walked out!"

"What did the man look like, Mr. Grove?" Nan inquired, her dark eyes shining with excitement.

When the museum man described his caller, Nan exclaimed, "He sounds exactly like the man we're looking for!"

All this time Arnold had been standing by, a bored expression on his face. "Why are you so excited?" he asked. "You can't do anything about him."

"Sure we can!" Bert protested. "We're pretty good detectives. We'll find the thief."

Arnold looked scornful. "I'm a better detective than any of you kids. Those jade figures your little sister was telling me about—I'll bet I can find them before you do!"

"They belong to a friend of ours, Arnold," Nan said indignantly. "And we're going to get them for her!"

"We sure are," Bert agreed with his twin. Then he made a suggestion. "But right now," he said, "let's go to the Honolulu police. I think we should report the story of Lani's treasure to them."

"All right," Nan agreed. "If the man who took the Pele stone is here, they should be able to find him!"

Mr. Bobbsey thought reporting the matter was a good idea. They thanked Mr. Grove for his kindness, then went out and climbed into the pink jeep.

When they reached police headquarters, the Bobbseys and Arnold were greeted by a sandy-haired officer who said his name was Lieutenant Mark Gilman. Mr. Bobbsey introduced himself and the children, then Bert and Nan told the officer about the stolen Polynesian relic.

He listened intently, then asked, "And you think this man you suspect of stealing the stone in Lakeport is here in Honolulu now? That's rather a long distance for him to have traveled, isn't it?"

"But we know he was in San Francisco," Nan said, "and our little sister was sure she saw him get on a plane there yesterday afternoon. He could have flown here."

"And from Mr. Grove's description of the man who came to the museum this morning, we think he's the same one," Bert added.

Lieutenant Gilman laughed. "You children are pretty good detectives. You almost have me convinced!" He rubbed his chin thoughtfully. "The man may be a Hawaiian. If he has been in any trouble in the islands we probably have his picture. Come with me."

Mr. Bobbsey and the children followed the officer into another room. "Here is our Rogues' Gallery," he said. "We'll look through these pictures. If any one of them resembles your man, let me know."

Officer Gilman placed several large albums on a table and began to leaf through them while Bert and Nan looked at each picture.

Suddenly Nan exclaimed, "There! That looks like him!" She pointed to the photograph of a deeply tanned young man with bushy black hair. "I could tell better if he was wearing thick dark glasses."

"Well, let's see what information we have on this man," the officer said.

He jotted down a number from the picture, then walked over to a file cabinet. In a minute he returned carrying a folder of papers. "It looks as if you may be right, Nan," he observed. "There's a notation in the description that the man normally wears thick dark glasses."

"What's his name?" Bert asked eagerly.

"Kamaki Slater. He was born here in Honolulu and is part Hawaiian. We have a long history on Mr. Slater."

"May we hear it?" Nan inquired.

"Well, it seems that he was mixed up with a group of men who were smuggling in antiques from the Orient. He was arrested, convicted, and served a term in prison."

"How long has he been free?" Bert wanted to know.

"Less than a year," the officer replied. "He disappeared from Honolulu and the rumor was that he had gone over to the Big Island, Hawaii. However, the police over there haven't seen him."

The policeman picked up a note pad and a pencil. "It's interesting to learn that he may be back in Honolulu. We'll make a search for him and let you know what we find out."

Mr. Bobbsey thanked the officer and led the way out to the jeep. Arnold had been quiet in the police station. Now he spoke up. "Have you been to Pali Pass, Mr. Bobbsey?" he asked.

"No, we haven't," Mr. Bobbsey replied. "What is it?"

"It's a pass through the mountains that divide this island into two parts. You can get a great view of the town on the other side of the island from the top."

"It sounds keen," Bert said enthusiastically. "Let's go, Dad!"

Following Arnold's directions, Mr. Bobbsey drove up the Nuuanu valley. They passed many beautiful homes set in luxuriant gardens which were bordered by hedges of small purple orchids. Coconut palms, as well as large green hau and monkey-pod trees, grew everywhere.

"Isn't Honolulu simply lovely?" Nan sighed. "I wish we could stay here a long time!"

The car had been climbing steadily. Now

jagged mountains rose on each side of the road. At last the jeep reached the top of the pass and Mr. Bobbsey pulled over into a parking area.

At one end, beyond a low stone wall, the ground dropped away a sheer two thousand feet. Far below the visitors could see a lush country of green fields and along the shore the low buildings of another community.

The children stepped out of the jeep and were met by a fierce gust of wind. "Oh!" Nan cried as her head scarf was blown off.

"I'll get it!" Bert called.

He ran after the bright cloth, but just then another gust of wind came. It caught the boy like a great wave. Bert was blown straight toward the low wall!

CHAPTER X

CHASE ON THE BEACH

"DADDY! Help!" Nan screamed as she saw her twin being blown toward the precipice. The wind was so strong that she could not move.

With a flying leap Mr. Bobbsey reached his son and grabbed him by the arm. They stopped just a few feet from the low wall. Then arm in arm they fought their way back against the terrific gusts.

"Thanks, Dad," Bert panted when he had climbed into the jeep again. "I really thought I was going over the cliff. I've never felt such a wind before!"

"You'd probably have been all right," Arnold said with a grin. "The natives around here tell a story about a man who tried to jump off this cliff. The wind was so strong that it blew him right back!"

"Some story!" Nan said with a shiver. "Let's go, Dad. This place scares me!"

When they reached the hotel again the Bobbseys found Mrs. Carson, the twins' mother, and the younger children having a late lunch in the outdoor dining room. Arnold went off to find his parents while the others sat down to report their morning's adventures, and how they had seen the Soda Shop man's picture at police headquarters.

"You really think the man we saw in Lakeport is Kamaki Slater?" Lani asked in surprise.

"We're practically certain of it," Bert replied, biting into a slice of juicy fresh pineapple.

"We're going to find him!" Nan asserted firmly.

"That's wonderful!" Lani exclaimed. "Now maybe I will get my treasure back!"

The children spent the afternoon playing tennis on the hotel courts. They had another refreshing swim, then dressed and met the grownups on a grassy terrace above the beach. Tables and chairs were placed in the shade of a huge keawe tree. The setting sun touched Diamond Head in the background with a mellow light.

Mrs. Bobbsey turned to Mrs. Carson. "This is really a lovely land, Jane. I don't wonder you like living here!"

"Look, Mother!" Nan whispered. "We're going to have some entertainment."

A man with a guitar, another with a ukulele, and three girl dancers took their places by the tree. The girls were dressed in white blouses and

The girl dancers took their places by the tree

skirts made of green ti leaves, the men in white shirts and slacks. All wore leis of brilliant red flowers.

The men began strumming a Hawaiian song and the girls started the graceful movements of a hula. Their long, dark hair and the green leaves of their skirts swung in time to the music.

The Bobbsey group was entranced by the grace and beauty of the dancers. Suddenly Nan became aware of amused glances in their direction from nearby tables.

Surprised, she looked around. There was Flossie, standing on her chair to see the entertainers better, and imitating the hand movements of the dancing girls! She was completely oblivious of any attention from her neighbors.

"Sit down, honey," Nan whispered. "You're disturbing people."

Suddenly noticing the smiles around her, Flossie blushed and slid down in her chair. But the professional entertainers had also seen the little girl. Now one of the hula dancers came through the crowd and stopped at the Bobbseys' table.

"You do the hand movements very well," she said, smiling at Flossie. "Won't you come up and dance with us?"

Flossie was embarrassed. She looked over at her mother. Mrs. Bobbsey nodded encouragingly and said, "Go ahead, dear, if you want to."

Taking the dancer's outstretched hand Flossie

skipped along beside her. When they reached the entertainers, the man with the ukulele slipped a lei around the little girl's neck.

During the next dance Flossie carefully watched the Hawaiian girl next to her and copied her movements. By the end of the number Flossie had caught on and when the music died away, there was a loud burst of applause from the audience.

"Say! You were good!" Freddie praised his twin when she returned to their table.

Flossie giggled. "It was fun hula dancing."

The next morning on the way to breakfast Freddie drew Flossie aside. "I've got an idea. Let's look for that Kamaki Slater."

"Oh yes, let's!" Flossie agreed. "Where shall we look?"

"I think everybody in Honolulu comes here to Waikiki Beach," Freddie observed. "I'll meet you when the others are getting ready for swimming and we'll walk up the beach. Maybe we'll see Kamaki."

Flossie nodded. Shortly after breakfast Mrs. Bobbsey suggested that everyone put on a bathing suit. Flossie explained to her that she and Freddie wanted to take a walk up the beach before swimming.

"All right," her mother said, "but don't be long."

The small twins started their trek through the

soft white sand. Now and then they stopped to examine unusual shells. Once Flossie called out, "Look at this, Freddie!" She stooped to pick up a piece of white rock covered with tiny holes. "See, it looks just like a lady's hand!"

A young man passing by heard her. Coming over to look at Flossie's find, he told her it was a piece of coral. "It does resemble a hand," he agreed.

"I'm going to take it back to Susie Larker," Flossie told her brother when the young man had walked away.

They strolled on, glancing at the people they passed on the beach. Suddenly Flossie grabbed Freddie's hand. "Look up there," she cried, pointing ahead to a group of sun-bathers. "Isn't that Kamaki?"

"I'm sure it is. I knew we'd find him!" the little boy said proudly. "Let's go closer. Maybe we can hear what he's saying."

Freddie and Flossie crept along and dropped down behind an overturned canoe. From this spot they could overhear the group's conversation. The tanned young man whom Flossie had noticed had black bushy hair and wore dark glasses. He was talking to three older men.

"How are things this season?" one of the men asked.

The tanned man shook his head and sighed. "I'm having much *pilikia* from the *malihini!*"

Freddie whispered, "That means he's having trouble with newcomers!"

Flossie's blue eyes grew wide. "Do you think he's talking about us?" she asked tensely.

At this moment the young man said, *"Aloha!"* to his companions and strode away in the opposite direction.

"Come on, let's follow him!" Freddie urged, springing to his feet.

Flossie joined him and they set out after the man. The suspect walked briskly along, calling *Aloha* to various people he met. Then he turned away from the beach and entered a grove of coconut palms.

"Hurry!" Freddie said desperately. "We'll lose him!"

The little twins began to run and reached the grove in a few seconds. They were just in time to see the young man enter a thatched hut at the edge of a clearing.

"Now what do we do?" Flossie stopped to catch her breath.

"There's a window in the side wall," Freddie observed. "Maybe we can peek in."

For a moment Flossie hung back. But her twin took her hand. "We've got to be *brave* detectives."

"All right, Freddie. I won't be 'fraid."

Quietly the small twins crept around to the side of the grass hut where Freddie had spotted the window. Standing on tiptoe, they tried to peer into the hut.

"It's too high!" Flossie whispered. "I can't see at all!"

Freddie looked around the clearing. At the base of a tall coconut palm there was a pile of palm fronds, evidently left there when the tree was trimmed.

"Maybe they'll help," he said.

Running over, Freddie began to drag a bunch of fronds to the hut. Flossie saw what he had in mind and hurried to help. In a few minutes they had a small heap of palm branches under the window.

Carefully the children climbed up. Now they could see through the half-open window into the interior of the hut. Surfboards leaned against the walls and there was a large canvas bin filled with bright colored beach balls.

To the twins' great surprise, the bushy-haired suspect was sitting on a stool varnishing a surfboard!

"Oh!" Flossie cried. "He can't be a thief!"

The man looked up, startled, and saw the two blond heads at the window. He jumped up and came outside.

"What's all this about a thief?" he asked pleasantly, a twinkle in his eyes. "Can I help you, little *malihini?*"

As soon as the young man smiled and spoke the

small twins, abashed, realized that he was not Kamaki Slater. Freddie gulped. "We—we're sorry we chased you and peeked in your window," he explained. "We thought you were the person we're looking for."

"Yes," Flossie joined in. "We're trying to find a man who has stolen something valuable. He has bushy black hair and dark glasses."

The young man's white teeth shone as he laughed heartily. "That's quite a job," he said. "All the beach boys along Waikiki have black hair and wear dark glasses—and thousands of people in Honolulu, too!"

Freddie and Flossie laughed with him. "I'm glad you're not Kamaki," Flossie announced. "You're too nice."

The friendly Hawaiian wished the children luck in their search, then Freddie and Flossie said good-by and hurried back to the hotel. They found Mr. Bobbsey and Lani waiting for them.

"I thought," said the twins' father, "that since Bert and Nan had a trip in the jeep yesterday, maybe you two and Lani would like to ride with me this morning."

"Oh, Daddy, that would be scrumptious!" Flossie cried, running up and throwing her arms about her father. "Where are we going?"

"I don't know," Mr. Bobbsey admitted. "Have you any suggestions, Lani?"

The little Hawaiian girl dimpled. "We might

drive around to see the Blow Hole," she replied.

"Blow Hole! What's that?" Freddie wanted to know.

"You'll see when we get there," Lani said mysteriously.

Mr. Bobbsey stopped at the hotel desk and received directions for reaching the spot. Then, with Freddie in front beside him and the two girls seated in the rear of the jeep, Mr. Bobbsey drove off. They went through the residential section around Diamond Head and then on alongside the blue ocean past Koko Head. When he saw a sign labeled "Blow Hole," Mr. Bobbsey pulled the car off the road into a parking space.

The children jumped out and started to scramble down the rocks between the road and the sea. Mr. Bobbsey followed.

"Where's the Blow Hole?" Freddie asked Lani.

She pointed to a group of lava rocks jutting out into the water. "Watch there!"

"I don't see anything," Freddie replied. Before anyone could stop him he ran over and climbed out on the rocks.

The little boy noticed a hole in one of them and bent over to examine it. At that moment a large wave thundered in from the Pacific. It surged into the space under the lava ledge. Then with a great *swish!* it rushed up through the hole in the rock in a huge geyser!

CHAPTER XI

A MEAN TRICK

FREDDIE was completely drenched by the geyser of sea water. "Glub, glub!" spluttered the little boy, shaking himself like a puppy.

Blinking, Freddie made his way along the rocks back to the others. He was soaked but grinning. "I had a shower bath!" he cried.

Flossie giggled. "Now you know what the Blow Hole is!" she teased.

"We'll have to take you back to the hotel and dry you out, my little fat fireman," his father said jokingly.

They all piled into the jeep again, and Mr. Bobbsey drove to Waikiki.

Later, when Freddie had changed his clothes and had lunch, he wandered past the tennis courts on his way to the beach. Arnold Cooper was there, lazily batting balls against the back net.

"Hi, Freddie!" he called. "How is your detective work getting along?"

Freddie looked glum. "Flossie and I thought we'd found Kamaki, but it was the wrong man," he said sadly. "I'm afraid we'll never get Lani's treasure back."

"I know where it is," Arnold said calmly.

"You do?" Freddie asked in amazement.

"Sure. Want me to show you?"

At that moment, Nan came up to the two boys. Freddie told her what Arnold had said.

"Where is the stone, Arnold?" Nan asked.

"I can't tell you. But if you want to come with me, I'll show you," the older boy replied.

Nan shook her head. "Why can't you tell us?" she asked, a note of doubt in her voice.

Arnold shrugged. "You'll just have to believe me. I thought you wanted to find Lani's treasure for her, but if you don't—!"

The blond lad picked up his tennis balls and sauntered off toward the hotel lobby.

"Oh Nan!" Freddie cried. "Let's go with him. I'm sure he knows where the Pele stone is!"

"We'll find Bert and see what he thinks," Nan suggested.

They went down to the beach where the other Bobbseys, Lani, and Mrs. Carson were basking in the sun. Nan explained to them what Arnold had told Freddie. "Do you think he's telling the truth?" she asked her twin.

"It's hard to say. You and Freddie might as well go with him and find out." Bert added that he could not accompany them. "Aka's coming to give me another surfing lesson."

"Yes, come on, Nan," Freddie insisted. "I'll get Arnold!" The little boy hurried away toward the hotel lobby.

Nan followed slowly. She still distrusted Arnold. But she did not want to miss any chance of returning Lani's treasure to her.

They found Arnold in the lobby scanning post cards on a rack. "Changed your minds?" he asked when Nan and Freddie came up.

"Yes," Nan replied. "We'd like you to show us where the Pele stone is."

"It's quite a distance from here," Arnold explained. "I'm not sure I feel like going that far right now." He turned back to the card rack.

"Please, Arnold," Freddie pleaded. "You said you'd take us!"

"Well, all right," the older boy answered reluctantly. "Follow me."

He walked down to the beach, then turned in the opposite direction from that which Freddie and Flossie had taken that morning. He led them along the sand and in a few minutes entered the grounds of a large hotel.

"Is the stone in here?" Freddie asked, surprised.

Without replying, Arnold guided them in a zig-zag course through the garden and came back onto the beach again. This happened twice more until Nan and Freddie were so mixed up they couldn't tell where they were.

Finally they came to a park-like spot. There were beautiful lawns and flowers. Scattered in among the trees were several nice-looking houses.

Nan looked around uneasily. Where could Arnold be taking them? She was more convinced than ever that the boy did not know anything about the whereabouts of the Pele stone.

In a few minutes the trio came to a large rectangular space bordered by a hedge of yellow-and-red-leafed crotons. To one side was a low white building.

Arnold stopped and pointed. "It's in there!" he said. Then he turned abruptly and ran off.

"Arnold! Where are you going?" Freddie called after him. The boy did not reply and soon had disappeared among the trees.

Freddie looked despairingly at his sister. "What'll we do now, Nan? Are we lost?"

His sister frowned. "I'm not sure. We might as well go in that building and see what it is."

The children walked across the grass to the low structure, opened the screen door, and went in. At a desk near the door sat a pleasant looking young man in a crisp Army uniform.

"What can I do for you two?" he asked with a smile.

"We're looking for Lani's stolen Pele stone," Freddie spoke up. "Is it here?"

The soldier looked puzzled. "No stone here, buddy." He looked at Nan. "What does he mean?"

"We were told that something which was stolen from a friend of ours was in here," she explained. "But I'm afraid the boy who told us was playing a trick on us."

"It looks that way," the soldier agreed. "This is an Army post."

"Oh dear!" Nan cried. "I guess we really are lost!"

When she told the young man where they were staying, he got up from the desk and walked into another room. In a few minutes he returned. A tall, weather-beaten soldier was with him.

"Hello there!" he boomed out. "The corporal here tells me we have two lost *malihini*. I'm going up the road in my truck. Would you like to ride with me?"

Freddie's eyes shone. "Yes sir!"

The man, whom the first soldier addressed as Sergeant Webster, led them out of the building and over to an Army truck parked nearby. First he lifted Freddie to the high seat and then helped Nan scramble up. Soon they had left the Army post and were driving toward the hotel.

When they reached it, the children jumped down and thanked the sergeant.

"That was super," Freddie told him. "I'm glad we got lost."

The Army man grinned, waved, and drove off.

Nan and Freddie reached the beach just as Bert was bringing in his surfboard. "Whew!" He dropped down on the sand. "Surfing is fun but I've sure fallen off a lot!"

His brother and sister sat down, too, and quickly told of how Arnold had tricked them.

"He really fooled me," Freddie said in disgust.

Bert clenched his fists angrily. "What a mean

thing to do! I guess you were right, Nan. He probably pulled those other tricks as you suspected! I'm going to find Mr. Smarty and teach him a lesson." Leaping to his feet, Bert ran to the Coopers' bungalow. He found the door open and the rooms empty. There was no sign of luggage.

"Arnold did say he and his mother and father were going to Hawaii," Bert thought. "Maybe they've already left. I'll go to the desk and see."

When Bert reached the hotel lobby, he saw Mr. and Mrs. Cooper at the desk. Arnold was lounging nearby. Bert strode up to the older boy. "That was a pretty sneaky trick you played on my sister and little brother!" he said hotly. "What was the big idea?"

Arnold edged away. "I haven't time to talk," he muttered. "We're going to fly to Hilo on Hawaii this afternoon. Maybe I'll see you there."

At this moment Mr. and Mrs. Cooper called their son. With a relieved look he followed them to a waiting car.

Bert stared after him, chagrined. But he shrugged his shoulders and made his way to the beach again. Nan and Lani were waiting for him. "Never mind about Arnold," she said. "Aka is going to take us all out in a real outrigger!"

Mr. and Mrs. Bobbsey and Mrs. Carson joined the children, and soon all eight visitors had taken their places in the long, narrow canoe. Aka was in the rear seat and with strong thrusts of his paddle sent the canoe out from the shore. When the others began to paddle too, they fairly flew over the blue water.

"This is great!" Freddie cried. "I wish we had someone to race."

Presently another canoe full of young boys drew near them. Aka explained that they were from a school nearby and had won many outrigger races.

"Let's challenge them," Bert suggested.

Everyone agreed, and Aka called out the invitation to the occupants of the other outrigger. The tanned boy in the rear replied, *"Ae,* but you will have to *wikiwiki* to beat us!"

Seeing the Bobbseys' puzzled faces, Aka explained, "He says yes, but we will have to hurry to beat them!"

The two outriggers were maneuvered into position parallel to each other, then Aka gave the signal. Down the paddles went, and the canoes sped forward.

"The outrigger which reaches a point opposite Ala Wai Canal wins!" Aka called to their opponents. Then he explained to his crew that the canal marked the end of Waikiki beach.

The Bobbsey craft had nine paddlers, but their six Hawaiian rivals in the other canoe were more experienced. They quickly pulled ahead.

Freddie grew alarmed. "Come on, Flossie," he cried. "Paddle harder!"

"I'll count," Bert proposed. "That will make our strokes even."

So, while Bert called out, "One, two, three, four," to the rhythm of the paddles, the outrigger spurted forward, each paddler stroking with all his might. Slowly they gained on the rival canoe. Then, side by side, the two craft raced through the water.

"The canal is just ahead!" Aka cried, catching the spirit of excitement.

With a final burst of energy, the crew of the Bobbsey canoe dipped their paddles deep and passed the Hawaiian group by half a length!

"Maikai loa!" the leader of the Hawaiian crew called. "Our *alohas* to you!"

"He says you are very good and his crew sends their love to you," Aka translated as the occupants of the other canoe waved and paddled on.

"That was fun!" Mrs. Carson exclaimed as they clambered from the outrigger at the hotel beach. "Lani and I will meet you when we've changed for dinner."

Later, seated around a large table under the hau tree on the dining terrace, the whole group discussed the outrigger race.

"I thought I'd burst when we passed the other canoe," said Freddie.

Just then a waiter appeared and announced, "Telephone call for Mrs. Carson."

"It's probably Frank," Mrs. Carson said as she rose from the table. "Excuse me."

In a few minutes she was back, her face pale and her lips trembling. "My husband has disappeared!" she cried.

CHAPTER XII

FIRE STEAM

"DISAPPEARED!" Mrs. Bobbsey echoed her friend. "Sit down, Jane, and tell us what happened."

Mrs. Carson explained that the call had been from Tracy Webber, one of the men at the Volcano Observatory. "He said that Frank went down into the Kilauea crater yesterday to make some scientific observations and hasn't come back."

"Oh Aunt Jane, how terrible!" Lani's brown eyes filled with tears.

"The Observatory men checked at our house, thinking perhaps Frank had gone straight home," Mrs. Carson continued, patting the little Hawaiian girl's hand. "When he wasn't there, Malia, our maid, suggested they call me here."

"I'm sure he's safe," Mrs. Bobbsey said comfortingly. "But you probably want to go right home."

When Mrs. Carson nodded miserably, Mr. Bobbsey got up. "I'll see what I can do about reservations," he offered.

He returned shortly with the news that he had made arrangements for the group to fly to Hawaii the following morning. The evening was spent packing for the next stage of their journey.

At the breakfast table, Nan said worriedly, "I want to help look for Mr. Carson, but I'm sorry to leave Honolulu without finding Kamaki."

Bert looked up. "I think we should call the police before we leave. We can give them our new address and at the same time hear if they have any news of the thief."

When the Bobbseys reached their rooms again, Bert put in the call. Nan stood by the telephone. Lieutenant Gilman came on the line and Bert told him their address on Hawaii.

"Have you heard anything about Kamaki?" Bert then asked.

There was some conversation on the other end of the line which brought a look of surprise to Bert's face. After a minute he thanked the officer and hung up.

"What did he say?" Nan asked eagerly.

"They haven't found Kamaki," Bert replied, "but Lieutenant Gilman says they've had a report from one of their policemen that he thinks he saw Kamaki jump on one of the inter-island boats just as it was pulling out."

"Where was the boat going?" Nan wanted to know.

"It goes all around the islands but it was scheduled to stop at Hilo, Hawaii, first. Lieutenant Gilman has notified the police in Hilo and they will try to pick up Kamaki when the boat docks there."

"I hope they catch him," Nan sighed. "But he's been awfully clever so far in getting away."

When the Bobbsey party boarded the plane a short while later they found the atmosphere on the two-engine craft very informal and pleasant. Their stewardess was a pretty Japanese-American girl with a friendly smile.

As soon as the plane was air-borne, she came back through the cabin bearing a tray with tall paper cups of fresh pineapple juice. "Have you been on the islands before?" she asked Nan, who had a seat next to Flossie.

Both girls shook their heads.

"Would you like to hear something about them?" the stewardess asked.

Freddie and Bert had seats across the aisle and they joined in the chorus of "Yes, please!"

The young woman perched on the arm of the seat where Mrs. Carson and Lani were, just behind the twins. "Honolulu is the capital of the state of Hawaii and, as you know, there are three other islands which tourists like to visit. Kauai is the farthest away from the mainland and is known as the Garden Island because of its lush tropical growth and beautiful gardens."

"It sounds lovely," Nan remarked.

"Then the island between Oahu and Hawaii," the stewardess continued, "is Maui. It is called the Valley Island because there is a valleylike isthmus separating the two mountain masses on each end."

"We're going to Hawaii," Flossie said. "It has two names, hasn't it?" She remembered that Mrs. Carson had said it was called the Big Island or the Volcano Island.

The young woman smiled. "That's right," she said. "It also has a third name."

"What's that?" asked Freddie.

"The Orchid Island. And you'll see why when you get there!"

"Look out the window, children," Mr. Bobbsey called. "We're nearing Hilo, Hawaii."

The plane was flying along the northern coast of the island now, and they could see the mountain ridges which ran down to the sea. Along the shore the water was a brilliant green turning to deep blue farther out. At intervals they could see green sugar-cane fields.

The pilot banked the aircraft, then the next minute, it seemed, the craft was down, rushing along the runway. Finally it came to a stop before the low airport building.

Mrs. Carson and Lani were the first off the

plane. Lani ran toward a wiry-looking man of medium height who wore a sombrero hat, blue jeans, and cowboy boots.

"Cowboy!" she cried.

When she reached him, the man picked her up and swung her high in the air. "Lani, we're glad to have you home!"

Then the man turned to Mrs. Carson. "We have no more news about Mr. Carson, but a party from the Observatory has gone into the crater and they should find him very soon."

Mrs. Carson smiled gratefully, then spoke to the Bobbseys. "This is Cowboy. He is part of our household. Cowboy has always lived on Hawaii and can answer any questions about it!"

Cowboy swept off his big hat and made a low bow. The children saw that he had twinkling brown eyes and a roguish grin. They liked him at once.

When they had all shaken hands with him, Cowboy walked over to a low stone wall and returned with an armload of beautiful orchid leis which he placed about the shoulders of each of the Bobbseys, Lani, and Mrs. Carson.

"Mahalo nui loa," Flossie said with a little giggle.

Cowboy looked at her and once more swept off his hat. "The little *malihini* speaks Hawaiian!" he exclaimed in delight.

"The leis are beautiful, Cowboy," Mrs. Bobb-

Cowboy looked at Flossie and swept off his hat

sey cried. "How many orchids does it take to make one?"

"Three hundred and fifty flowers in each lei," Cowboy explained proudly. "They are grown here. That is why Hawaii is known as the Orchid Island."

The group followed Cowboy to a large station wagon and all piled in. After about an hour's drive through sugar-cane fields and groves of tropical trees, they arrived at the Carsons' house. It was set among tall trees, and a wide porch ran around three sides of the house.

As the car drove up, a middle-aged Hawaiian woman came out to greet them. She was plump and smiling. Her dark hair was wound around her head in braids, and her brown eyes sparkled with friendliness.

"This is Malia," Mrs. Carson explained. "She is pure Hawaiian and can tell you many stories of our island."

"But now you must be hungry," Malia said. "I have teriyaki burger for your lunch."

Lani squealed in delight. "Wonderful!" She turned to the Bobbseys. "You'll love it. It's made of meat soaked in soy sauce."

The Bobbseys did like the spicy taste of the meat, and Freddie had two servings. "I'm going to take a piece of teriyaki burger back to Teddy Blake in Lakeport," he announced, and everyone laughed.

"How is the volcano, Malia?" Lani asked.

The Hawaiian woman shook her head. "Pele is restless," she said. "There will be an eruption soon."

"Why do you say that?" Nan inquired.

"I can tell," Malia replied mysteriously. "It always happens when Pele is about to send an eruption!"

"What happens?" Bert asked.

Malia folded her hands and looked very serious. "The other night," she began, "my brother was driving to Hilo when he had a flat tire. He got out to change it and was starting to work when he realized he did not have his wrench. Suddenly someone put it in his outstretched hand. He turned around quickly, but of course there was no one there!"

"Who was it?" Flossie asked eagerly.

Malia shook her head and shrugged her shoulders. "Who knows? Perhaps Pele. In any case there will be an eruption soon. It is the sign."

Mrs. Carson smiled at Malia's superstitious tale. Then she grew sad. "If there is going to be an eruption, I hope they find Frank before it happens," she said. Then she brightened. "But Frank knows every inch of that crater. He can't be lost for long."

After lunch the Bobbseys unpacked and then their hostess suggested that Cowboy would drive them around the island a bit.

"I think Richard and I would like to stay here with you until you hear from Frank," Mrs. Bobbsey observed, "but I'm sure the children would love to go."

So the twins and Lani started out with Cowboy at the wheel. Freddie and Flossie sat in front with him, and the older children in the rear.

"Why do they call you Cowboy?" Freddie asked as they turned onto the main road.

Cowboy explained that he had once worked on the Parker Ranch on Hawaii, but had grown tired of handling cattle and so had taken a job with Mr. Carson.

"The Parker Ranch is a wonderful place," he went on. "It's the second largest in the United States. But I always thought I'd like to be nearer Kilauea, so here I am!"

"Look at the ferns!" Nan exclaimed. The road now wound between banks of giant ferns, as tall as trees. They rose green and feathery on both sides of the drive.

"This is called the Fern Forest," Cowboy said. "We're on the eastern slope of Kilauea now."

"You mean we're on the volcano?" Nan asked in amazement, looking around at the green growth.

"That's right," the driver assured her. "In a minute we'll come to the crater."

Now they were out of the forest and driving

along a plateau. Cowboy parked the car by the side of the road and got out. "Come see a volcano," he said. "And I'll show you some queer things."

The children followed their guide across the ground. He paused. "Look down there," he said. "That's the inside of the volcano."

There was a wide crack in the barren ground and far below the children could see a swirling, bubbling mass of something which looked like mud.

"Ugh!" Flossie exclaimed. "What is it?"

"Molten rock," Cowboy answered. "And it also contains gases. Come over here and I'll show you something else."

The children followed him toward a spot where they could see steam issuing from the ground. Cowboy stopped at a circular pit about six feet across. Several feet down they could see water.

Freddie wrinkled his nose. "It smells bad!" he commented.

Cowboy smiled and took a box of matches from his jeans. "Watch this," he said.

He struck the match and tossed it into the pit. Instead of being extinguished by the water the lighted match caused a small explosion. Tiny red and yellow flames shot up above the ground.

"Ooh!" cried Flossie, pulling back.

"What makes the fire?" Bert asked curiously.

Cowboy explained that hydrogen sulfide gas formed below the surface of the earth and escaped in the form of steam. When it came into contact with fire, the fumes ignited.

"Is that what causes volcanoes to erupt?" Nan inquired.

"Something like that," Cowboy replied. "When the gases in the earth's center build up to the point where they cannot find a release, they explode and an eruption occurs. The combination of molten rock and gas is called magma when it is underground and lava when it pours out onto the surface."

Lani clapped her hands. "You sound just like Uncle Frank, Cowboy!"

Flossie had grown a little restless with all the talk about volcanoes. Now she spoke up. "Are we near the Cave of Refuge, Cowboy?"

Their guide replied that it was not far away and would be their next stop. They got back into the car and after a short drive Cowboy turned off the main road onto one which led toward the sea.

He parked the car near several others full of tourists. As the children got out and started toward the beach they heard a shout from one of the cars. Arnold Cooper was waving to them.

Then he cupped his hands to his mouth and called, "You're too late! I found them!"

CHAPTER XIII

THE CAMEL ROCK

"FOUND what?" Flossie asked in bewilderment. "What does Arnold mean?"

Nan had an idea, but she didn't want to alarm the younger twins. "He's probably just trying to tease us," Nan said.

Bert understood his twin and winked in agreement. Besides, Arnold probably *was* teasing.

The children decided to pay no attention to the boy.

Nan noticed several booths set up under the trees. "Oh, look at the pretty jewelry!" she said.

The tables were spread with a collection of necklaces, earrings, and bracelets made of shells, seeds, and carved ivory.

By one of the displays stood a stout Hawaiian woman. Her brown hair was piled on top of her head and around her neck she wore a lei of fragrant white jasmine blossoms.

"Come see my jewelry," she called.

Nan and Lani ran over to the table and were soon admiring a necklace and earrings made of ivory carved into the shape of the jasmine flower.

"I have some money with me," Lani said. "I'm going to get that set for Aunt Jane."

"And I'll buy one like it for Mother!" Nan exclaimed.

While the girls were busy at the jewelry table Freddie and Flossie had caught sight of two plump little Hawaiian children playing under a nearby tree. The twins ran over and had soon started a lively conversation.

Nan and Lani picked up their purchases and Nan called, "Come on, Freddie and Flossie! We're going down to the beach!"

The small twins said good-by to their new friends, and Flossie ran up to her big sister. "They're *mahoe* too. That's twins in Hawaiian!"

Bert and Cowboy had already gone to the beach and the others followed. When they reached the sand, Flossie stopped short. "Why, it's black!" she exclaimed in amazement.

"That's another sign of the volcano," Cowboy said. Then he explained that when the hot lava from a volcanic eruption met the cool water of the ocean it exploded into fragments of black glass. The action of the waves through the years ground these fragments into fine black sand.

"Where is the Cave of Refuge?" Flossie asked, looking around.

"Just down the shore to the right," Cowboy pointed out. "But why are you so interested in it, little *malihini?*"

Flossie explained about the buried jade toys which they had promised to find for their friend in Lakeport.

Cowboy nodded thoughtfully. "There were lots of cases like that in the old days, I hear. I hope your jade is still there."

"What does the Cave of Refuge mean?" Freddie asked.

Lani explained. "It was called the Cave of Refuge because in the early days if a person who had done something wrong could make his way to the cave, he would be safe from punishment."

"Flossie and I ought to have a Cave of Refuge at home," Freddie remarked with a grin.

Bert laughed and ruffled his little brother's yellow hair. "You do pretty well without one!" he teased.

Then he looked along the shoreline. "It must have been around here that Captain Phinney buried the jade figures. Remember, we have to find a tree near a rock which looks like a camel!"

"There are lots of funny-looking rocks," Freddie observed. "I think it must be down this way." He started along the beach.

"No, it's up the other way," Flossie declared positively.

Nan laughed. "I suggest we divide and search.

One group go up the shore, the other down. Come on, Lani, you and I will follow Freddie."

They started up the beach, while Bert and Flossie turned in the opposite direction. The shoreline was covered with rocks of black lava twisted into many weird shapes.

Flossie ran on ahead of Bert. Suddenly she sat down with a sharp cry. Bert hurried up to her.

"What's the matter?" he asked anxiously.

"I stepped on a rock and turned my foot," she explained, "but the hurt is almost gone!"

"Sit still a minute," Bert advised. "Then if it isn't better, I'll carry you back to the car."

Flossie rubbed her foot and looked pensively out to sea. Then she sat up straight, a look of excitement on her face. "There it is!" she pointed to a lava formation a short distance out in the water.

Bert looked. "I don't see it," he said. "Where? Then he moved to a spot directly behind Flossie and peered out over the sand. "Now I get it! Say, that sure does look exactly like a camel with a hump on its back!"

At their shouts the others came running up. They, too, recognized the camel, but Nan said doubtfully, "The captain's letter sounded as if the rock was on the beach—and where is the tree?"

"That's right," Freddie agreed. "This must be the wrong rock!"

"There it is!" Flossie exclaimed

Lani spoke up. "The captain wrote his letter many years ago and I've heard that the beaches on the islands are all getting narrower because of the waves pounding against them. It could be that this rock was once on the beach."

"I think you've got something, Lani," Bert agreed. He glanced around. "And there's a tree at the edge of the beach which could be the one the captain meant."

"Let's dig around the tree and see if the jade figures are buried there!" Flossie proposed excitedly.

"What can we use to dig with?" Bert asked thoughtfully.

Lani came to the rescue. "I'm sure Cowboy will have something in the car," she said. "I'll go see!"

She ran off with Bert by her side. In a few minutes they were back, Bert carrying a garden hoe.

"This was all Cowboy could find," Lani explained. "He had just had it repaired, but he says we may use it."

"That's fine," Nan said. "We can take turns digging."

Just then Cowboy came strolling along the beach strumming a ukulele. When the Bobbseys exclaimed, he told them that he never went anywhere without his ukulele.

"I also have a guitar and a violin in the back

of the car," he added. "I play them all and entertain myself. Would you like me to play for you while you dig for your treasure?"

When the children all eagerly agreed, he sat down beneath a tree, leaned back against the trunk, and began to pluck the strings of his ukulele.

"That's pretty," said Flossie. It was a lovely Hawaiian melody.

It was decided that Nan and Bert would start the digging. Nan was the first to take the hoe. To her surprise the dirt was soft and she went to work with a will while Cowboy strummed on his instrument and sang songs which he had learned on the Parker ranch.

"It's your turn now," Nan said to Bert after a few minutes. She passed the hoe to her twin.

One after another the children took turns digging but without finding anything. Then Flossie turned over some earth and suddenly bent over to examine it more closely.

"I see something sparkling!" she cried.

The other children dropped to their knees around her and quickly began to push away the loose dirt. Freddie held up a piece of thin wood.

"That looks like the top of a cigar box!" Cowboy exclaimed, taking it from Freddie.

"And here's the rest of it!" Nan said excitedly, holding up a dirt-stained box. "The hoe must have broken it open!"

All round in the dirt the children began to pick up small, shiny, black beads. "What are these, Cowboy?" Nan asked.

"They're really bits of lava," was the reply, "but they're called Pele's tears and some folks made necklaces from them."

"They're like the stones the plane stewardess told us the sailors found in Diamond Head," Lani reminded Nan.

Bert had picked up several small pieces of rock and was examining them curiously. He was interested in minerals and had a collection of them at home in Lakeport.

Cowboy took the pieces from him. "See these bits of brownish-green stone?" he asked. When Bert nodded, he went on, "They're called olivines and jewelers are glad to buy them. They're really lava too, but when they're taken out of the surrounding rock, cut and polished, they make very handsome semi-precious stones."

"This is really volcano land," Nan observed. "All sorts of beautiful things come from the volcanoes."

"Do you suppose Nellie's great-great-grandfather buried these stones too?" Flossie asked.

Bert shook his head thoughtfully. "No, I don't," he said. "You saw how easy it was to turn over this earth? For that reason, I'm sure this box hasn't been buried very long!"

"But who could have put it here?" Nan asked.

"Someone who expected to come back for the box very soon and didn't want to carry it around," Cowboy guessed.

"What shall we do with the stones?" Lani wanted to know.

Cowboy said that he would take them to the police and that if the lava pieces were not claimed they would be given to the children who had found them.

"Oh goody!" Flossie clapped her hands. Then her face grew sober. "But where are Nellie's jade figures?" she asked.

"I thought so," Nan cried suddenly. "Arnold found the jade and took it!"

CHAPTER XIV

TRACKS IN THE CRATER

NAN'S statement that Arnold probably had dug up the buried jade figures made Bert shake his head.

"I don't think he'd be able to locate the figures so quickly," Bert said soothingly. "When Flossie told him about them she didn't mention the camel-shaped rock. He wouldn't have known where to dig."

"I hope you're right," Nan replied gloomily. "But remember when we were in the Honolulu museum, Arnold said he'd find the jade before we did!"

"Arnold can't have it," Flossie wailed. "I promised Nellie we'd bring the toys back to her!"

"No, he can't!" Freddie declared.

Cowboy said they must leave now. Nan put an arm around her little sister and tried to comfort her as they sadly walked back to the car.

When they reached the Carsons' home again

the children learned that the search party had returned from the crater without finding Mr. Carson. "Everything's gone wrong today," Lani wailed.

"Tracy Webber is going to continue the search tomorrow," Mrs. Carson explained, trying to appear cheerful.

"I'm sure they'll find him on the next trip, Jane," Mrs. Bobbsey said consolingly.

When Mrs. Carson had left the room, Mr. Bobbsey said to his wife, "I met Webber this afternoon and volunteered to go with the party tomorrow. He accepted my offer."

"Good, Richard!" Mrs. Bobbsey approved. "I know Jane will be glad."

"I wish we could help look for Mr. Carson," Nan said wistfully.

"Oh yes! May we go with you?" Lani looked imploringly at Mr. Bobbsey.

"I'm afraid it's too dangerous for the children, Richard," Mrs. Bobbsey protested.

"The men from the observatory are very careful and well-trained, Mary," her husband explained. "I think it would be perfectly safe."

"We would do just what they told us to," Bert added pleadingly.

Mrs. Bobbsey smiled. "All right, then."

"I'll call Webber and ask him about bringing you on the expedition tomorrow," the twins' father offered. "I can tell him that you children are very good at finding people and things!"

"But we didn't find the little jade figures!" Flossie reminded him of their failure at the beach.

Nan told her parents about meeting Arnold and of his boast. Bert added, "We're going to search around that part of the shore again when we have the chance."

Mr. Bobbsey went to the telephone and returned with the news that Tracy Webber would be glad to have the older children join the search party.

"But I'm afraid Freddie and Flossie will have to stay at home this time," he said. "I'm sure you two can find something to play with around here."

"I know Cowboy would like to take you swimming," Lani spoke up.

Although disappointed, the younger twins agreed that it would be fun to go with Cowboy. "Maybe he'll teach us some songs!" Freddie remarked in an attempt to cheer up Flossie.

Early the next morning, Mr. Bobbsey and the three children went outside. Tracy Webber arrived in a jeep driven by another man from the observatory. Mr. Webber was tall and blond with rather a stern look. But when he smiled the twins decided that he was very nice.

"Jim's going to let us out at the rim of the crater," the scientist explained. "With four such good helpers as I'm sure you Bobbseys and Lani will prove to be, I decided we shan't need him and he can go back."

In a short while the jeep stopped at the end of the crater and the passengers piled out. Tracy Webber carried a knapsack with water and first-aid supplies, while Mr. Bobbsey had a light bed-roll slung across his shoulder. The children had packages of sandwiches.

"I'll take the lead and we'll walk single file," Mr. Webber announced. "Lani will come after me, then Bert, Nan, and you, Richard."

As they fell into line, he added, "Just follow me. If you don't go wandering off on your own we'll be all right."

The first part of the way was quite steep and the searching party slipped and slid down the incline. After a while the walking grew easier. The floor of the crater was covered with a thin layer of pumice fragments, remnants of lava fountains of a hundred years before. Here and there were blocks of old lava, some of them several feet across.

Suddenly Lani cried out and stooped to pick up a small leather notebook which had been wedged part way under a large lava block.

Mr. Webber turned around. "What is it, Lani?" he asked. "Have you found something?"

The Hawaiian girl held out the notebook. "It's Uncle Frank's!" she cried.

"Are you sure?" the scientist asked. "Let's look at it!"

He took the small book and opened it. Then he let out a jubilant cry. "It is Frank's! And there's a message!"

"How wonderful!" Nan exclaimed. "What does it say?"

Mr. Webber read:

"I think I have broken my ankle. An old Hawaiian has found me. He does not speak English but from the way he points I think he is taking me to his home on the volcano slope. Will whoever finds this please notify the Observatory?"

"That's lucky," Mr. Bobbsey said. "Evidently he's not in too bad shape. Have you any idea what direction we should take, Tracy?"

The volcanologist took off his broad-brimmed hat and scratched his head thoughtfully. "Well now, let's see," he began.

Bert's sharp eyes had spotted something in the crater dust. "Look, Mr. Webber!" he called. "These tracks could have been made by somebody dragging a foot!" He pointed to faint marks in the cinders.

"By Jove, I think you're right!" the scientist exclaimed. "We'll try to follow them. If they were made by Carson and the Hawaiian, they should lead us to the spot where the men left the crater."

The trail was dim and hard to see in the dust.

Nan spotted a small grass hut

Sometimes they lost it completely when crusted lava covered the ground. But they managed each time to pick it up again.

The party progressed slowly across the crater floor, then into a ravine which finally led them to a wooded area on the outside slope of the volcano.

Nan spotted a small grass hut nestled among the trees. "Maybe Mr. Carson's in there!" she guessed, and began to run toward it. The others followed.

When they reached the open door of the shack, Lani peered in. Then she cried out happily, "Uncle Frank! We've found you!"

The others followed Lani into the hut. There on a low cot lay Frank Carson. His face, covered by a three days' growth of beard, looked wan and haggard. But when Lani threw her arms around him, he smiled gratefully.

"I don't know how you got here," he said wearily, "but I'm certainly glad to see you! Kaula has fixed me up pretty well, but he refused to leave me to go for help. I was beginning to think I'd never get away from this hut."

Mr. Carter looked over at a huge Hawaiian who crouched on the floor before a small fire. Hearing his name, the man looked up with a flashing smile and shook his head.

"Tell us what happened, Frank," Mr. Bobbsey urged. "How long have you been here?"

"Three days," was the reply.

Then Mr. Carson told his story. He had started out early one morning to make some scientific observations in the volcano crater. About noon he had slipped and injured his ankle. He had been sitting on the block of lava wondering what to do when the Hawaiian, Kaula, had come along.

"He practically carried me here to his house, put a splint on my ankle, and has been caring for me ever since. But the only thing he says which I can understand is 'Pele! Pele!' Then he looks toward the crater and shakes his head!"

At the words Kaula walked to the door, peered up at the sky, and muttered, "Pele!"

Tracy Webber bent and examined the injured man's ankle. "Kaula's done a good job there," he reported. "Now all we have to do is get you back home."

"I can speak Hawaiian," Lani reminded the group. "Is there something you'd like me to say to Kaula?"

"Yes," Tracy Webber replied. "Ask him how far we are from the road."

There was a short conversation in Hawaiian, then Lani reported that Kaula had lived all his life in the woods. He had gone out only to buy a few necessities. "He says the road is about two hours from here," she ended.

Mr. Webber pondered a minute, then suggested, "If Kaula will guide me to the road, I can get some help for Carson. Perhaps Lani should come too so she can talk to Kaula for me. You Bobbseys stay and look after Frank."

"Wouldn't you like something to eat before you leave?" Nan asked, opening the packages of food.

The scientist agreed that this was a good idea. Kaula quickly laid out some polished coconut shells. They all sat on the floor and hungrily munched on the roast beef and chicken sandwiches which Malia had prepared. Even Kaula was persuaded to eat, although he still muttered uneasily.

They had just finished the last bite when there was a loud *boom* in the distance. The sky beyond the open door turned an orange red!

Tracy Webber jumped to his feet. "The eruption!" he shouted. "It's begun!"

The Hawaiian ran to the door, wringing his hands and screaming, "Pele! Pele!" He was shaking with fear.

The Observatory man acted quickly. He began to unroll the rubber mattress which Mr. Bobbsey had brought. "We can't wait to bring help. We'll have to leave now!"

Bert sprang to his assistance. "We can carry Mr. Carson on this!" Mr. Webber nodded.

In the meantime Mr. Bobbsey had gone over to Kaula and had managed to quiet him. With Lani's help he made the Hawaiian understand that they must leave the hut at once. He led the man to the mattress upon which Mr. Carson was now lying and motioned for him to pick up one corner.

"Good for you, Richard," Frank Carson commented. "We've got to make Kaula come with us. I was afraid he would refuse to leave the volcano."

The Hawaiian, however, seemed content to go with the group. With Mr. Webber, Mr. Bobbsey, and Kaula each holding one corner of the bedroll, and the children taking turns at the fourth, the party started down the narrow ravine away from the crater.

It was hard going. The single path ran between the steep sides of the ravine, and it was difficult to carry the mattress without tipping it. Behind them the group could hear the roar of the unseen volcano and a strange crackling noise which the volcanologists explained was the sound of trees exploding from the heat of the eruption.

When they stopped to rest for a minute, Nan pointed back and exclaimed, "Look! A fountain of fire!"

Far off through the trees they could see a giant spray of red-hot pieces of lava being tossed high into the air. The odor of sulphur reached their nostrils and dried their throats. Mr. Webber passed the thermos of water and they each poured a paper cupful to quench their thirsts.

After a minute, Mr. Webber called, "All right, let's go!"

They picked up the mattress and trudged on, listening uneasily to the roar of the volcano behind them. Suddenly Tracy Webber looked back.

"The flow is coming this way!" he shouted. "We're in its path!"

CHAPTER XV

A RACE WITH THE LAVA

THE others stopped and turned around. What a sight met their eyes! A river of flame was creeping down the ravine. It slid slowly forward like a giant snake, accompanied by the crackling of trees as the heat struck the bark.

Mr. Webber glanced hastily around him. "We must get out of here fast!" he exclaimed.

Frank Carson raised up on one elbow. "I think I know where we are now," he said. "A little farther on is a spot where we can climb up the side of the ravine. If we can reach higher ground, we'll be safe."

"Good!" Webber agreed. "We'll push on then."

The men picked up Mr. Carson once more, this time with Bert taking the fourth corner of the mattress.

"We're lucky in one way," Mr. Carson observed. "We're far enough away from the actual eruption to miss that hail of lava rock."

141

"Yes," Tracy Webber agreed. "It's falling back into the crater and then spilling out through this ravine. It's a good thing we weren't any nearer."

The group hurried forward, with a glance behind them now and then at the slowly advancing lava flow. Ahead the road was rocky and they had difficulty keeping their footing.

Nan and Lani scrambled along behind the others. Suddenly Lani stepped on a sharp stone, lost her balance and pitched forward. She struck her head and for a moment lay stunned in the path.

"Lani!" Nan cried, rushing to her side.

Hearing the girl's cry, the four carrying Mr. Carson set down the mattress. Bert dashed back to his twin. Between them they helped Lani to her feet. But she was still dazed and wobbled uncertainly.

Taking in the situation, Tracy Webber joined them and quickly examined the little Hawaiian girl.

"There doesn't seem to be anything seriously wrong," he decided. "I think she's just shocked. If you twins can help her, we three men can manage Carson."

"Sure we can," Bert said quickly.

"Let's make a chair," Nan suggested, "and we can carry Lani until she feels better."

Bert agreed. The twins grasped each other's

The twins urged Lani to take her place on the
improvised seat

wrists and urged Lani to take her place on the improvised seat. When she was safely settled they followed the others. Kaula, the large Hawaiian, by gestures had made Mr. Webber and Mr. Bobbsey understand that he could carry the front of the mattress while the other two took the rear corners.

They had walked only a short way when Mr. Carson called out, "This is the spot! I think we can make it up the side here."

Lani said she felt all right now. She jumped down from the seat, insisting that she could walk by herself. When the children joined the adults Frank Carson struggled up from the mattress.

"We haven't any time to lose," he insisted. "You could never carry me up that hill on the bedroll. If you'll all just give me a push when I need it, I'm sure I can manage."

In spite of protests from the others, he stood up and hobbled to the side of the path. Then, pulling himself up by grasping the branches of some low trees, he began the ascent of the steep slope.

Kaula bounded to Carson's side and with his strong arms almost lifted the scientist from tree to tree. The group had left the path not a minute too soon. The lava had now almost reached the spot where the party had begun the hillside climb. It was growing hotter and hotter.

"Whew!" Bert exclaimed. "This heat is terrific!"

"It certainly is," his perspiring father agreed breathlessly.

The sky which they could glimpse through the trees had an eerie orange glow. The underbrush along the path had caught fire and sent a choking smoke up toward the climbers.

At last they dragged themselves up to the road which ran around the rim of the crater. Everyone was gasping for breath and water streamed from their eyes because of the sulphur fumes.

"Are you all right, Uncle Frank?" Lani asked anxiously as the volcanologist sank down onto a large rock.

"Yes," he replied wearily. "But I think I'll wait here until some of you can bring help."

Bert peered up the road. "Here comes a car!" he exclaimed.

Lani ran out into the road and waved her arms. "It's Cowboy!" she explained. "He's come to get us!"

The station wagon pulled to a stop beside Lani, and Cowboy's grinning face appeared at the window. "Anybody like a ride?" he asked jovially.

Then he saw Mr. Carson seated on the rock and quickly got out of the car. "Oh, I'm sure glad to see you, sir!" he cried out. "But you're hurt!" he said with concern.

Mr. Carson explained about his injury and the driver helped him into the car. When the others turned to thank Kaula they discovered that he had already started back to the ravine. Bert hurried after him, but the big Hawaiian shook his head stubbornly.

"Lani!" Bert called. "Come tell Kaula he can't go back to his cabin while the volcano is erupting!"

Lani ran over to the Hawaiian and talked earnestly to him. In a few minutes, however, she was back, and Kaula had turned into the woods.

"He says he is a friend of Pele's and must go back. She would be very angry if he left his home," Lani explained.

"As a matter of fact," Mr. Carson conceded, "I don't think the lava or the fire will reach his cabin. He'll probably be perfectly safe."

"Mahalo nui loa!" Nan called after the man. He smiled and waved as he disappeared among the trees.

"Cowboy," said Lani, "how did you happen to be driving along the road at this time?"

He told her that when the eruption had begun he had started out to look for the search party. "It sure is lucky I came along here at just the right moment!" he said.

The ride to the Carsons' house did not take long, and the appearance of the group was greeted with great joy by those at home. Mrs. Carson hastened to call a doctor to examine her husband's injured ankle. He was soon in bed resting from his painful experience.

As Tracy Webber started to leave, he paused. "How would you all like to come to the Volcano House and watch the eruption?"

He explained that the Volcano House was a hotel situated on the rim of the crater. The National Park Headquarters was very near.

"Oh, yes, Mother!" Flossie cried. "Freddie and I haven't seen the 'ruption at all!"

Mrs. Bobbsey laughingly agreed to their going. Mrs. Carson and Lani decided to remain at home, but the Bobbsey family piled into the car with Cowboy and Mr. Webber and drove to the Volcano House.

Crowds of people had already arrived when they reached the attractive hotel built on the very edge of the volcano crater. The terrace in front of the building was filled with visitors. Many had binoculars and telescopes focused on the active volcano.

"I thought volcanoes were dangerous," Freddie said in wonder, "but nobody is running away from this one!"

Cowboy laughed. "That's right, Freddie," he said. "Volcanoes are tourist attractions in Hawaii. As soon as there's word of an eruption, everyone runs to look at it!"

The view from the terrace was an awesome

one. From where the Bobbseys stood they could see two fountains tossing red-hot lava hundreds of feet into the air with a tremendous roar. The lava fell into the crater forming fiery pools which in turn spilled over the rim in crimson torrents.

Suddenly a Park Ranger standing nearby raised a megaphone and shouted, "Back, everyone! Off the terrace!"

The wind had shifted and a shower of hot cinders began to fall as the crowd scattered. When the Bobbseys reached the shelter of the hotel lounge, Mrs. Bobbsey looked around. "Where is Flossie?" she cried. "I thought she was with you, Nan!"

"She was until we got to the door and then we were separated by the crowd," Nan replied. "I'll find her!" She dashed off.

In a few minutes she was back, holding her little sister by the hand. In Flossie's other arm was a tiny white poodle with a pink hair ribbon tied on its topknot.

"Flossie!" her mother exclaimed. "Where did you get the dog?"

"Just outside by the door. He was all by himself," Flossie explained. "I was afraid maybe Pele would take him away!"

From across the big room came a frantic cry, "Poof-poof! Where are you, darling?"

The little dog wriggled from Flossie's arms.

He ran across the room and was greeted with exclamations of joy by a large blond woman in a Hawaiian muumuu. She called to Flossie, "Thank you for saving my precious. I was frantic."

Mr. Webber laughed. "Good for you, Flossie. Now, I must get back to the Observatory." He thanked the older twins and Mr. Bobbsey for their part in the morning's rescue and went off in a Park jeep.

Cowboy drove the others back to the Carsons' home, passing long lines of cars making their way to the Volcano House to watch the eruption.

When the Bobbseys reached the house, they found a very excited Malia. "There have been strange happenings around here!" she told the twins.

"What kind, Malia?" Nan asked curiously. "Tell us about them."

The maid shook her head worriedly. "Pele is angry. I don't want to be mixed up in it. You must ask Lani!"

The children went off in search of the Hawaiian girl and found her at Mr. Carson's bedside.

"Oh, I've been waiting for you!" she exclaimed when they came into the room. "Kamaki Slater must be here on Hawaii!"

"Why do you think so?" Nan asked excitedly.

Lani held out a crumpled piece of paper. "This was wrapped around a piece of lava rock we found on the porch," she explained. "Read it!"

Nan took the paper and in a trembling voice she read aloud:

"Pele is angry that her stone has been stolen. If you want it, leave money under large rock at entrance to lava tube tonight. Otherwise it will be returned to Pele!"

CHAPTER XVI

THE PLAY MONEY SCHEME

"WHAT kind of tube is a lava tube?" Freddie asked when they had all heard the message. He looked confused.

"And how could there be a rock at the entrance of a tube?" Flossie chimed in. "A tube isn't very big."

"A lava tube is!" Mr. Carson laughed and explained that there were two kinds of lava: *pahoehoe* which was smooth, and *aa* which had a rough surface. "During an eruption the *pahoehoe* soon crusts over and forms a roof. At the end of the eruption most of the molten *aa* lava drains out from the main tube, leaving a tunnel."

"A tunnel!" Bert exclaimed. "How big is it?"

"Have you ever been in a subway?" the scientist asked.

When Bert assured him that all the Bobbseys had ridden subways in New York City, Mr. Carson continued, "Well, these lava tubes look some-

what like a subway tunnel. They're about fifteen
feet high, with an arched roof and a flat floor."

"If there is more than one lava tube," Nan
said, "how do we know which one the thief
means?"

"The Thurston Lava Tube not far from here is
the most famous one," Mr. Carson replied. "I'd
guess that's the one."

"But what are we going to do?" Lani asked
anxiously. "I do hope I can get my sacred stone
back!"

Mr. Bobbsey had come into the room during
the discussion. Now he spoke. "I think we'd better phone the police and tell them the whole
story. Then we'll do whatever they advise."

"I'll make the call," Bert offered. When his
father nodded, he and Nan ran from the room.

Bert's call was answered by an officer who
identified himself as Captain Kim. The man was
told about the theft of the Pele stone in Lakeport;
the mix-up in trying to catch the thief in the
park there; and the failure to get in touch with
him in San Francisco. Bert finished by reading
the note left at the Carsons' home.

"And you think this thief is Kamaki Slater?"
the captain asked.

"Yes, Captain Kim." Bert explained about the
resemblance between Slater and the man in the
Soda Shop.

"Lieutenant Gilman phoned me from Honolulu about Kamaki," the officer said. "But we haven't seen any sign of him here on Hawaii."

"What shall we do about this note?" Bert asked the officer.

The man was silent for several seconds, then said, "I'd suggest you follow the same plan you did in Lakeport. Leave fake money. I'll be in the tube tonight and will nab the fellow."

Nan whispered to Bert, "Ask him if we may go along."

Bert passed on the request. "Of course," came the hearty response. "I'll stop and pick you up when it gets dark."

The twins returned to Mr. Carson's room and reported their conversation. It was decided to make up the fake package and conceal it under the rock that afternoon.

"Freddie and I want to see the lava tube!" Flossie cried, and her twin agreed.

Nan looked at Mr. Carson. "Could Cowboy take them to the tube?" she asked. "They could hide the money while they're there."

Mr. Carson nodded, and Lani ran off to get Cowboy. When the children told him about the note and their plan to leave fake money at the lava tube, he grinned.

"You *malihinis* are real detectives! I'd sure like to help fool that guy who stole Lani's Pele stone. You just get that money ready and Freddie, Flossie, and I'll hide it for you."

Lani ran off and returned with a large sheet of wrapping paper. "Will this do?" she asked.

Mr. Bobbsey took a bill from his wallet. "Here," he said, "measure by this."

Lani drew an outline of the bill on the paper. Then she, Bert, and Nan carefully cut out a dozen pieces of the same size. "That should make a real-looking bundle if we put it in an envelope," Bert observed.

Cowboy brought a long white envelope, and the make-believe "bills" were slipped inside. Then he said, "All right, Freddie and Flossie, let's go!"

With Freddie clutching the fake money, the small twins climbed into the front seat of the station wagon and Cowboy drove off. In a short while he stopped along a wooded road.

"Here we are!" he announced. "See that opening there to the left? That's the entrance to the lava tube."

The twins jumped out and Cowboy drove on to a clearing where he parked the car.

"Come on, let's go in," Freddie cried, grabbing Flossie by the hand.

The little girl hung back. "I think we should wait for Cowboy," she said.

"He'll be right here," Freddie insisted. "Come on!"

When they reached the entrance, Flossie stopped. "Oh! It's so dark!" she exclaimed. After

"Oh! It's so dark!" Flossie exclaimed

the bright sunlight the tunnel was inky black.

But Freddie pulled her by the hand and they crept cautiously ahead into the darkness. Suddenly, two small gleaming lights appeared in front of them.

Flossie stopped with a scream. "Wh-what's that?" she quavered.

"What's what?" Freddie asked. Then he saw them too. "I-I think they're an animal's eyes!"

"A bear?" Flossie whispered.

"I'm not sure there are bears in Hawaii," her twin answered doubtfully. He moved forward a little. As he did so, the eyes came closer.

Flossie turned to run. At the entrance of the tunnel she saw a flickering torch. "Cowboy!" she screamed.

The driver ran forward. "What's the matter?" he cried. "Are you hurt?"

"N-no," Flossie replied, "but—"

Freddie came running back to Cowboy. "There's a wild animal in there," he announced.

"What!" The man shone his torch about. There at the side of the tunnel crouched a little animal. It had gray fur, a long tail, and looked like a small cat.

When Cowboy stepped forward the creature scurried away. "That's a mongoose," he explained. "He won't hurt you. The sugar planters brought them here to the islands years ago to kill the rats in the sugar-cane fields."

Flossie spoke up quickly. "What kind of a goose is a mon-goose?" she asked. "He had four legs. A goose-goose has only two!"

Cowboy laughed. "I don't know why they're called mongooses. They're more like ferrets than geese. Mongooses are good little animals to have around."

Freddie looked admiringly at Cowboy's torch. "That's a keen light!" he said.

The man explained that it was a typical Hawaiian torch. The light was made by burning oil from the kukui nuts in the container. Holding the torch high, he led the children through the tunnel and back again to the entrance.

"That was scary," Flossie said with a little shudder, "but fun!"

"Now let's hide the money!" Cowboy suggested.

Freddie looked startled, then turned pale. "I don't know where it is," he stammered.

"You were carrying it," Flossie reminded him. "Did you leave it in the car?"

The station wagon was searched and the ground all around the entrance to the tunnel, but no sign of the envelope containing the fake money could be found.

"Perhaps you dropped it in the lava tube," Cowboy suggested.

He lighted the torch again and led the way into the tunnel. The flickering flame of the torch cast weird shadows on the lava rock walls. Flossie took Cowboy's hand.

The three walked the length of the tunnel, then turned back. "I don't see it anywhere," Flossie said. "Do you s'pose Kamaki followed us and found it?"

At that moment the light caught a glimmer of white. Cowboy stooped and picked up the envelope! "This is just about where you saw the mongoose," he observed. "I guess he startled you so much that you dropped it then."

"Thank you, Cowboy," Freddie cried. "I'm awfully sorry I lost the money. May I be the one to hide it?"

Flossie and Cowboy agreed, so when they came out of the lava tube Freddie looked around for the rock. Just to the right of the entrance he saw a tall, moss-covered stone. There was a small hollow in the ground just in front of it.

"This must be the rock the man meant," Freddie remarked. Stooping, he slid the envelope into the hollow and far enough under the rock so that it would not blow away.

Flossie looked around with a little shiver of excitement. "Do you think Kamaki is here somewhere and is watching us?" she whispered.

"Oh, I hope not," Freddie replied. "He's not supposed to come until night so Bert and Nan can catch him!"

Cowboy drove Freddie and Flossie back to the

Carsons, then left them with a promise to be on hand early the next morning to learn what had happened. The small twins entertained the others at dinner with an account of their adventure with the mongoose.

"And two of them are called mongooses, not mongeese," Flossie reported with a giggle. "And they won't hurt you, even if I was scared by one of them."

Everyone laughed, then Mrs. Carson said with a smile, "You must remember that there are no wild animals or poisonous snakes on Hawaii."

It seemed to Bert and Nan a long time before darkness fell, but finally Freddie and Flossie went sleepily off to bed. Shortly after that a police car drove up with Captain Kim at the wheel.

"This is Lieutenant Murato," he explained, introducing his companion, a short, slim man with sleek black hair. "He knows Kamaki and will be able to identify him if we make our capture."

Lani had begged to go along so she, Bert, and Nan piled into the back of the police car. Captain Kim stopped his automobile some distance from the lava tube. He drove into a small clearing and parked where a tangle of bushes would hide the car from the road.

"We'll walk from here," he explained. "I don't want the suspect to see any car around when he comes to pick up the money."

Single file, the group walked in the dirt along the edge of the pavement so their footsteps would not be heard by anyone in the vicinity. When they reached the lava tube, Captain Kim motioned the children into the tunnel ahead of him.

"Murato and I will stay here near the entrance," he directed. "You children stand behind us. I don't want you in the way if there's any trouble."

Bert, Nan, and Lani followed directions and walked a little way into the tunnel. They stumbled in the darkness, then at Lieutenant Murato's signal crouched down against the wall. A faint light came from the entrance and they could see the two officers silhouetted at one side of the opening.

The group waited in silence for what seemed like a long time. The only sound was the rustle of some tiny animal in the underbrush and an occasional sleepy bird call. Then the watchers heard a different noise.

"Here he comes!" Bert breathed in Nan's ear.

Holding their breaths, the children could hear footsteps. Captain Kim and Lieutenant Murato shifted their positions slightly. Again there was silence.

"He must have gone away," Nan murmured in disappointment.

But in a few seconds the sound came again, and this time the children saw a shadowy figure pass in front of the tunnel entrance. It stopped and appeared to be looking around. Then the dark form melted into the surrounding darkness.

At that moment a beam of light sprang from the tube opening. It struck the figure of a man kneeling in front of the tall rock. The envelope of fake money was in his hand.

"The Soda Shop man!" Nan exclaimed.

CHAPTER XVII

CAPTURED!

"KAMAKI," Lieutenant Murato called out, "you're under arrest!"

Bert and Nan looked at each other in triumph. So the man they had seen in the Soda Shop and Kamaki Slater *were* the same person!

"What's the matter?" Kamaki asked sullenly as he straightened up. "I haven't done anything!"

"Oh no?" Captain Kim spoke as he snapped handcuffs on the man's wrists. "What about writing a letter demanding money dishonestly?"

"I don't know what you're talking about!"

Bert had pulled the note from his pocket. "Don't you recognize this?" he asked.

"Okay. So I wrote it! You can't arrest me for that!" Kamaki said roughly.

"We'll see about that," Captain Kim replied. "Maybe at headquarters you'll feel more like talking."

During this conversation Lieutenant Murato

had slipped away and now drove up in the police car. The captain shoved the prisoner into the back seat and climbed in beside him.

"Bert, suppose you come in with me," he instructed. "The girls will sit in front with the lieutenant."

As they started off Bert turned to talk to Kamaki. "We saw you that day in the Lakeport Soda Shop," he observed. "What were you doing there?"

The man said nothing. The captain smiled. "You might as well answer, Slater. These children know all about your record and that you've been in prison for smuggling."

"I was in Lakeport trying to get in touch with some pals of mine," the man admitted.

"And you overheard Lani telling us about her Pele stone, didn't you?" Nan asked from the front seat.

Slater admitted that he had heard Lani's story and been very interested in it. Since he was part Hawaiian himself, he knew about Pele, the volcano goddess. He realized that anything connected with her which had been handed down through so many years would be very valuable.

"So you made up your mind to steal it, didn't you?" Nan accused him.

"I was going to give it back," Kamaki blurted, "but that other kid messed everything up when I came to the park to collect."

"That was Danny Rugg," Bert explained to Captain Kim. "He's always spoiling things for us."

"Then I read in the local paper that the Bobbseys and Lani Kahakua were going to San Francisco and Hawaii," the prisoner went on. "I wanted to get back here anyhow, so I followed you."

"Then you were in San Francisco and took a plane at the same time we did!" Bert observed.

"Yes, but you could have had the stone that night in Chinatown, if you hadn't been so smart and let the police in on it!" Kamaki said defiantly. "I recognized Lieutenant Pratt and got out of that restaurant fast!"

The prisoner admitted that he was the one who had tried to sell the valuable relic to the museum in Honolulu. "But that curator wanted to know too much!"

"Okay, Kamaki," Captain Kim said. "You've been cooperating pretty well. Give us back the Pele figure and maybe we can make things easier for you."

The thief looked thoughtful, then said, "It's in my shack. If you want to take me there, I'll get it for you."

"Where is this shack?"

"Down by the Black Sand Beach. It was empty, so I just took it over," he replied with a smirk.

Following Kamaki's directions, Lieutenant Murato drove along for a few minutes, then turned down a side road.

"Stop here!" the prisoner called out. "The shack's down by the beach. We'll have to walk the rest of the way."

The moon had come up, and by its light the group could see the outline of a grass hut about halfway between the road and the sea.

When the car stopped, Kamaki in a sudden movement managed to open the door by him in spite of his handcuffed hands. In a flash he was out of the car and running.

The escape was so sudden that for a moment nobody did anything but stand still in amazement. Then Captain Kim snapped on his flash and by its light they saw the thief run toward the beach. Both Captain Kim and Lieutenant Murato took up the chase.

"I'll head him off!" Bert called, and ran directly toward the ocean.

Kamaki was thrown off guard by these tactics. As he saw Bert coming at him, he swerved to avoid the boy. This slowed his pace. Seizing the opportunity, Bert stuck out his foot and tripped the fugitive. He fell flat on his face!

"Here he is!" Bert shouted. "I've caught him!"

When the police officers arrived they found Bert seated on the prisoner's back.

Bert stuck out his foot and tripped the fugitive

"Thanks, my boy," Captain Kim said. "That was quick thinking!" Then, nudging Kamaki with his foot, he went on: "All right, cut out the funny stuff, and get us that stone!"

The thief got up slowly. Lieutenant Murato, holding him by one arm, led the way to the shack. Kamaki motioned toward an oil lamp which stood on a rough wooden table. When Captain Kim had lighted it, the one room of the grass house was illuminated.

"Okay. Where is the stone?" he asked.

In one corner of the room lay a dilapidated sleeping bag. Kamaki knelt by this and after much fumbling drew out an object wrapped in newspaper.

The police captain took it and removed the covering. Inside was the reddish stone piece which Lani had shown to the Bobbseys in Lakeport!

"We've found it! We've found it!" Nan cried excitedly.

In the dimly lighted room the Pele stone seemed to give off a soft glow. As Lani gazed at it tears came to her eyes. But she smiled happily, exclaiming, "It's my Pele stone! Oh, I'm so happy!"

Captain Kim replaced the wrapping and tucked the package under his arm. "I'll have to take this with me now as evidence, but we'll see that nothing happens to it. Come on, it's time you children were in bed. You've done a good job tonight."

When the officers let Bert, Nan, and Lani out at the Carsons' home a short while later the grownups greeted them with questions. "Was your evening a success?" Mrs. Bobbsey asked as they came into the living room.

"Oh yes! I found my Pele stone!" Lani cried happily.

"I'm so glad," Mrs. Carson exclaimed. "I know how upset you were to lose it. Now, I suggest we go to bed and in the morning when Freddie and Flossie are awake you can tell us all about your adventure!"

The children were tired enough to agree and soon were fast asleep.

Freddie and Flossie were the first ones at the breakfast table the next morning, eager to hear what had happened the night before.

"We found my treasure!" Lani told them at once.

Malia, who was serving the scrambled eggs at that moment, put down the platter. "I knew it!" she exclaimed. "Pele is satisfied and happy now and the eruption has stopped!"

"By George, you're right, Malia!" Mr. Carson said. "They called me early this morning from the observatory to say that all the activity has ceased."

"I hope Kaula is safe!" Nan said.

"He is," Mr. Carson assured her. "Tracy Webber told me that they had checked. His hut was not in the path of the lava flow and the fire didn't reach there."

"Oh, I'm so glad," said Nan.

She and Bert and Lani took turns describing for the small twins and the grownups the exciting events of the previous night. "And Bert was a real hero!" Lani said enthusiastically. "He kept Kamaki from getting away!"

"I wish Freddie and I had been there," Flossie said wistfully. Then she brightened. "But we put the money in the right place!"

"Yes, you did," Nan agreed. "You and Freddie had a very important part in catching the thief!"

At that moment the telephone rang. Malia answered it, then came into the room to say that the call was for Bert. When he returned, Bert said:

"Captain Kim wants us children to come to headquarters. We have to identify Kamaki and the Pele stone for the police records."

"I'll drive you in," Mrs. Carson volunteered. "I want all of you to see some more of the sights on our island."

The formalities at police headquarters were brief. Lani identified the ancient stone as her property and told the story of its theft.

Then Kamaki Slater was brought in. Lani and all the twins were sure he was the same man they had seen in the Lakeport Soda Shop and this was put into the record.

When they were preparing to leave, Freddie had a sudden idea. "Do you suppose Kamaki had anything to do with the box of stones we found at the Black Sand Beach?" he asked Flossie.

"He might have," Flossie replied, wide-eyed. "Nan said that hut where he was living was near the beach!"

The little twins drew Lieutenant Murato aside and told him of their find a couple of days before and their suspicion that Kamaki might have buried the stones.

"I remember that case," the lieutenant said. "Cowboy brought the stones and left them here in your names as the finders. Ask Kamaki about them if you want to."

Freddie stepped up to the prisoner who was still standing sullenly between two guards. "Did you hide a box of volcano stones on the Black Sand Beach?" the little boy asked.

"Yes I did!" the man answered. "And they belong to me. A pal of mine collected them after an eruption a couple of years ago. He gave them to me to sell on the mainland when I go back. I buried them for safekeeping."

"I suppose they're yours if you can prove your story," the officer said grudgingly, "but if you can't, they'll go to the Bobbsey twins as the finders!"

The prisoner sneered as he was led back to the jail. The Bobbseys, with Mrs. Carson and Lani, said good-by to the police officers and started for the parking lot where their car had been left.

As Bert and Nan crossed the street, they heard a shout from behind them. They turned around and saw Arnold Cooper just coming out of a shop.

Nan went back to him. "Arnold," she said determinedly, "tell me the truth. Did you find the jade figures we told you about?"

The boy looked annoyed. "No," he replied, "and you won't either. The place is buried in lava!"

CHAPTER XVIII

Aloha, Mahoe!

"BURIED in lava! It can't be!" Nan cried.

"Well, it is! Go see for yourself," Arnold said rudely. "I've just been out there and it's all covered."

Bert and Nan were dismayed. They said good-by to Arnold and got in the car with the others. Nan repeated what the boy had said.

"I don't believe it," Freddie spoke up.

But Flossie shook her head sadly. "Nellie will never get her jade figures now."

Mrs. Carson was sympathetic. To cheer her guests, she said, "Why don't you get Cowboy to drive you over there after lunch? You might be interested in seeing the effects of a fresh lava flow, anyway. It does queer things sometimes."

"Like *not* covering things?" Freddie asked hopefully.

"Yes, even that."

Cowboy was seated in the kitchen with Malia,

strumming on his guitar, when the group reached home. He readily agreed to drive the children to the Cave of Refuge again.

When Flossie told him they had discovered who had buried the lava stones, Cowboy shook his head in amazement. "You kids are the best detectives I've ever known," he exclaimed. "I sure hope the police give you those olivines and Pele's tears. You deserve them!"

After lunch the children piled in the car and drove off with Cowboy. When he reached the Black Sand Beach he parked the car and they walked down to the ocean. They began to retrace their steps to the camel-shaped rock.

As they rounded a little curve in the shoreline a scene of desolation met their eyes! A wide stream of black lava reached from the water up the slope as far as they could see. It looked like a frozen river of black ice. It was still steaming here and there, and the air was full of sulphur fumes.

Freddie began to run toward the lava. "I'm going to skate on it!" he declared.

Cowboy dashed after him. "Come back here!" he cried. "You'll burn your feet. Even though that lava has already hardened, its temperature is still about two hundred degrees!"

Freddie looked startled and backed away from the black river. "Thanks for stopping me, Cowboy. I thought it would be cold, not hot!"

"Isn't that the place where we dug?" Nan asked, pointing to a spot near the beach.

There stood the tree. Its top was gone and the trunk looked as if it had turned into black stone.

"It's weird looking," Lani remarked. "We call them tree molds. They're formed when *pahoehoe* lava surrounds a tree. It gets hard while the tree inside burns away."

"And after a time," Cowboy took up the story, "the charcoal and ash inside blow away and leave a hole in the lava where the tree once was."

"It's sort of spooky-looking," Nan said with a shudder.

"I see what Arnold meant," Bert observed. "No one can dig under that tree now!"

"Yes," Nan agreed. "I guess Captain Phinney's jade is buried forever!"

Freddie walked back up the beach a short distance to an area which had escaped the lava flow. Now he stopped and looked thoughtfully out to sea. He was still in line with the camel-shaped rock.

"Maybe that wasn't the right tree after all," he mused. "Perhaps Captain Phinney's tree has blown down since he was here so long ago."

He looked around. There was a tree stump just back from the sand. The stump seemed old and was overgrown with vines. Freddie peered out toward the water again. The queer rock was still in his line of sight.

"Flossie! Bert! Nan!" he yelled. "Maybe that was the wrong tree. Why don't we dig under this one?" When the other children ran up, Freddie explained his idea.

"Can't hurt to try," Cowboy said. "That hoe is still in the car. I'll get it."

He went off and in a few minutes returned with the garden implement. Once more the children took turns digging up the earth. When they had made a large hole at one side of the stump without finding anything, Bert stood back and mopped his forehead.

"I don't think this is the right tree either," he said in discouragement.

Lani looked thoughtful. "You know, if this is the tree, maybe the captain would think it safer to bury his treasure on the side away from the water."

"I see what you mean!" Bert replied. "Let's try the inland side."

They set to work again with a will and presently, when Freddie had the hoe, there came a *clink* of metal.

"You've hit something!" Flossie cried, hopping on first one foot, then the other. "Hurry, hurry! Let's see what it is!"

Frantically the children pushed the dirt aside until a rusted iron box about a foot square was revealed. Bert leaned over and with Cowboy's help lifted it from the hole.

The lock was rusty, but Cowboy pulled a penknife from his pocket and with one blow knocked off the hasp. Then he handed the box to Bert.

"I'm so 'cited!" Flossie exclaimed. "Open it!"

Bert put the heavy box down on the stump and gingerly raised the lid. The interior was filled with little packages wrapped in yellowed newspapers.

"Look! They're Chinese papers!" Lani cried, recognizing the special black characters.

Bert lifted the packages out and handed one to each of the children. They opened them eagerly. Nan was first to see hers.

"How darling!" she exclaimed in delight as she unwrapped the jade figure of a little old man carrying a parasol.

"And look at this!" Lani held up a water buffalo carved from white jade.

In turn Freddie, Flossie, and Bert discovered a strange-looking dog, a long-legged bird, and a tiny ricksha, all made of jade.

"They're mighty fine pieces," Cowboy remarked.

"Captain Phinney must have had fun picking these out for his children," Nan said. "Isn't it a shame they never saw the toys?"

"But Nellie Parks will have them now!" Flossie reminded her. "Let's send her a post card right away that we've found her treasure!"

Cowboy drove home through a little town and

the twins selected a post card showing the beach with the black sand.

"Let's say 'X marks the spot,'" Flossie suggested with a giggle as Nan addressed the card and licked on an airmail stamp.

"I'll put it in the box!" Freddie cried, taking the postal from Nan. He made a big X, then drew a little picture of a box in the margin of the card. "Now she'll see exactly where her treasure was," he said.

The card was mailed, then they drove back to the Carsons' house. When they showed their discovery to the grownups, Mrs. Carson exclaimed, "Just think how long these figures have been in the ground! And it took the Bobbsey twins from the mainland to uncover them!"

"I'm glad they found them today," Mr. Bobbsey said, "because we have to leave here tomorrow!"

"Oh no, Daddy!" Flossie wailed. "Why?"

"I've had word about a business transaction which means I'll have to get back to Lakeport quickly. I've made reservations for us to fly home tomorrow," her father explained.

"So tonight is your last night with us," Mrs. Carson said sadly. "Malia wants each of you to tell her your favorite Hawaiian food and she will try to have it for dinner."

Freddie spoke up at once. "I'll have teriyaki burger," he said. "That's what I like best."

Mrs. Carson laughed. "That's easy. How about you, Nan?"

"Malia's coconut pudding is my favorite," Nan answered.

Bert voted for sticks of fresh pineapple, and Flossie piped up, "I like the ice cream made from those macadamy nuts."

"I think you mean macadamia nuts," Mrs. Bobbsey corrected her. "I agree with Flossie!"

That evening after they had enjoyed Malia's delicious dinner, everyone moved out to the patio. Cowboy brought his guitar and began to strum some plaintive Hawaiian melodies.

"Look!" Nan whispered to Bert.

Malia had slipped into the patio and was dancing a hula. She wore a muumuu and her long brown hair hung down her back. Over one ear she had fastened a huge yellow hibiscus flower.

When Cowboy realized that Malia was dancing to his music, he played faster. Malia kept up with him and began to sing a song in Hawaiian which made Cowboy and Lani laugh.

"There are funny hulas as well as romantic ones," she explained to the Bobbseys. "This one tells a story about a little boy and his trick pig that did somersaults."

Malia and Cowboy completed their entertainment by singing a lovely old Hawaiian song, then the twins and Lani went off to bed.

The next morning the Bobbseys said good-by

to Mr. Carson and wished him a speedy recovery.

Then Cowboy drove Mrs. Carson, Lani, and their guests to the Hilo airport where the Bobbseys would board a plane to Honolulu.

As they drove up to the low building, Bert nudged Nan. "Look!" he said. "There's Arnold!"

The boy was standing nearby with his parents. When he saw the Bobbseys, he called, "Are you going back to the mainland?"

As the twins nodded, Arnold said, "Maybe I'll see you there." He followed his father and mother through the gate toward a waiting plane.

"Not if we see you first!" Bert muttered to his twin.

Nan giggled. "He's almost as bad as Danny Rugg. I'm glad we're not going on the same flight!"

As she and the others stepped out of the car, Cowboy winked at Lani and the two disappeared into the airport building. In the few minutes, just as the visitors were waiting to go through the gate, they reappeared. Their arms were laden with beautiful leis of plumeria, jasmine, and orchids.

Lani placed one of the flower garlands around the shoulders of each of the Bobbseys and cried, *"Aloha, mahoe!* Good-by twins! Come back soon!"

They all replied, *"Aloha! Aloha!"*

Flossie turned as she went up the steps into the plane and called back, *"Mahalo nui loa!"* Then she added, *"Aloha,* Volcano Land!"